MW01153994

Fact - Did you know that **Florida** was named by explorer Ponce de Leon in 1513? Ponce de Leon was searching for the Fountain of Youth and was told by Native Americans that the Fountain of Youth could restore youth to anyone. The name **Florida** comes from the Spanish word "florido", which means "full of flowers", or "flowery." Cite: State Symbols USA.

Fact - **The Florida State Bird** is the Northern Mockingbird and the **Florida State Flower** is the Orange Blossom. **State Tree** is the Sabal Palm.

Fact - According to Guinness World Record, the animal species with the most names is the Cougar and has over 40 names in the English language alone. This includes the Puma, Ghost Cat, Shadow Cat, Mountain Lion, Painter, Mountain Screamer, Panther and Catamount.

ISBN: 9781072267850

She Slipped

UNDER THE BLUE RAINBOW

by

JEAN BELEW – SILVER

CHAPTER 1

Introduction - June 7, 1536 in Wilderness Florida – the entire Timucuan village felt the vibrations from the warm meteorite that sizzled past them and crashed violently, without mercy, into trees, rocks, and caves with a reverberating sound and billowing mounds of dust. Every settlement and Indian Village in wilderness Florida for miles around felt the vibrations. They all said they had seen the large flash in the sky and heard the loud boom. Even the Calusas, further on down the state, said they had also felt the strange tremors coming from the ground.

For a fact, it was a frightful day when the meteorite smashed every unlucky thing in its path. The inhabitants of that land hid in fear until only the bravest came out to investigate the unusual events and to announce that it was indeed safe to venture outside their huts again. Even the animals were in a state of panic and unrest until things subsided; they all ran in a chaotic jumble of uncertainty, each in different directions trying to get to safety. It was quite an event.

The inhabitants could not even imagine what had caused such a thing to happen. However, over time, they got used to the big rock that had crashed too close to their villages. Actually, the impact was so intense that it was partially buried in a heap of dirt and ashes deep into the ground beside the mouth of a cave; a few fragments had scattered and fell to the ground in other places.

There were several long tunnels inside the opening of the dark cave; these tunnels led to other chambers that were filled with bats and insects. Most people stayed away from the cave, at least for a while anyway. Eventually, after a few years, certain people started coming to the cave to take advantage of the cool waters that had sprung up around the rocks.

The story begins on April 19, 2017 - almost 500 years after the meteorite hit Florida -

"Hey Josh, give me a hand with this canoe," Danica shouted from the shed when she saw him come out back and onto the lanai.

"Sure, not a problem, but where's Grandpa? I didn't see him in the house," Josh yelled back.

"He's over there at the worm bed getting us a few worms for bait." She pointed towards the back of the property where their grandpa had his vermicomposting bin set up.

Danica had to smile at the 'worm hobby' of their grandpa's. Now that he was retired from the Navy, he was beginning to do some interesting things that Danica had never seen him do before, like the 'worm hobby'. Before retirement, he was just too busy for things like that, but now he was supplying the whole neighborhood with free worms for fishing, or so it seemed.

She was proud of their Ex-Navy SEAL grandpa and found it a little amusing to see him get so involved with raising these worms. However, it did sadden her to see that arthritis was painful for him these days, and it made life difficult by slowing him down tremendously.

As she thought back on things, she did realize what a positive influence he had been in her life, and he did teach her some cool things about survival and the use of different weapons. They went to the shooting range often, and Danica became skilled at 'shooting sports' as a recreational activity and used various types of ranged weapons with accuracy and speed.

Her grandpa would say, 'Just so you'll know how to take care of yourself.' He would chuckle and make a joke about it. 'While you're out looking for dinner, you don't want to become dinner.'

She turned her attention back to the dusty and cluttered shed. "Boy, what a mess! I have to definitely clean this shed soon for Grandpa."

Josh walked over to the shed and leaned in to get a closer look. "Wow, that looks pretty bad. Just let me know when you're ready and I'll help you clean it."

They saw their grandpa slowly coming towards them with some worms that were desperately trying to get out of a paper cup.

Josh waved. "Hey Grandpa, whatcha got there?"

"I've got some worms for you. Look at that one right there on the top; he just won't stay in there. Look how fat he is." He was laughing now and was clearly amused with his new hobby and seemed to enjoy pushing the worm back down into the cup with his finger.

"Hey Danica, get a look at these worms." Josh motioned for Danica to lean in closer to see. They both lingered there making a big deal over the worms because they knew it was important to their aging grandpa.

"Nice. Those are some healthy worms you have there Grandpa," Danica smiled. It made her happy to see that the worms gave him something to do outside the house these days, and some much-needed exercise. She sadly remembered when he used to power-lift, and he had loved almost any kind of sport. She made herself a promise to try and get him to go with her on some short walks over to the park. Some more exercise and a little fresh air wouldn't hurt him. He used to enjoy walking over there to take photos of the numerous types of birds that were so common to this area, and portions of the park were directly beside the river that also ran behind their house.

"I fed the worms table scraps; that's what made them so fat."

Danica heard the enthusiasm in his voice but she knew his energy was waning. She also heard the way he was huffing and puffing as he had walked over to them.

"Interesting." Danica looked into the cup and lingered there as if the *worms* were the most important thing happening these days. Her heart warmed then at that thought and realized that nothing was more important to her than her aging grandpa and her cousin Josh. She couldn't resist the urge to reach over and give her grandpa a big hug and said, "I really missed you Grandpa."

"I missed you too baby."

"Wow, look, they're getting out of the cup," Josh said.

"I'd better get something bigger to put these in," Grandpa said.

A few minutes later, their grandpa held out a larger container. "Here, this will be better and you two go have some fun. I'm going back inside; I'm a little tired."

Danica hugged her grandpa again and said, "You do that and try to rest."

"I will." He turned to go back towards the lanai and all at the same time he held his hand up in a short wave.

"See ya Grandpa." Josh waved and dumped the worms over into the larger container.

Danica watched in silence as he slowly walked back into the house and all the while she was thinking about *what a bitch old age must be.*

She had just come back home to Tampa two days before, and the airport was buzzing with activity. She noticed that they had stepped up security by having airport police in places that was more visible. Seeing them carry AR-15 semi-automatic rifles was a comforting feeling to her because of the unrest around the world these days. One of the officers came really close to where she was standing in line and the no nonsense look on his face seemed to say 'don't even try it'. She felt even more secure than before and wondered if the people milling around even realized that he was there for their protection. *Who knows? Oh well, I hope they do,* she thought.

Anyway, she was glad to be back home and had really missed her grandpa these last four years while she had been away in the Army. She had missed Josh too; they were best friends and first cousins. To be even more exact, they lived next door to each other on the Hillsborough River in Florida, and conveniently, they lived just a few houses down from a quiet and peaceful park. To Danica it was a relief to be away from the heavy traffic and the blasting horns that dominated the congested highways in this area.

Danica had moved in with their grandparents when her mother had passed away from an unexpected heart attack when she was only eight years old. Danica had to deal with many anxicty attacks after that while trying to adjust to her mother's death. Josh and Danica's mothers had been sisters and were very close, and as a result, Josh was more like a little brother to her, except now he was no longer little, he was 6'3" and she was 5'8". She had never minded him tagging along everywhere she went, and who could complain, he was the only one that loved canoeing as much as she did.

She sighed now, remembering that her own dad was what her mother had referred to as the sperm donor because he didn't even stay around for marriage, or Danica's birth. She never knew him, but she did feel a definite void there with no father at all. All she knew about him was that he had been stationed at the Air Force base and never even looked back to say goodbye. Danica knew it was hurtful for her mother, so as a result, she didn't even bother to try to contact him and knew she never would.

"Gross, look at the dust." Josh's voice brought her attention back to the task of getting the canoe ready to put into the water again. "Hey, quit daydreaming and come over here and help me."

"Yep, got it." She grabbed one end and they both lifted it out and onto the grass.

"So, where's Jordan today? I thought she might want to go with us." Danica was eager to see her too.

Josh laughed. "You know she's not going to mess her pretty hair up and get all sweaty. God forbid."

"Oh, okay, I just thought I'd ask." She fondly smiled too because they both knew that Jordan would maintain her well-kept appearance at all costs, with one exception – kickboxing – because that firmed the buns, aka gluteus maximus. Danica and Jordan both found that sport exhilarating and a good way to burn calories and tone muscles.

In their teenage years, they would sit and talk for hours about anything of interest that day. They experimented with makeup and nail polish until they found just the right one to match up with their outfits. It didn't matter what they talked about, their conversations usually went back to clothes, jewelry, perfumes, shoes, moisturizing lotions, music, boys, and eventually the most interesting boy that Danica thought a lot about was Alex. Yes, Alex, that disastrous crush that had a crash and burn ending.

They also talked a lot about what they wanted to do when they got out of school, and it was not to Danica's surprise when Jordan decided to open an upscale and fashionable dress shop. Joining the Army seemed like the natural thing for Danica to do because she was already comfortable with firearms, and she admitted it outright, that she wanted to see more of the world than Tampa. Well, that she did, but now she was ready to be back home and ready to decide what to do with the rest of her life.

Josh's voice brought her attention back to the present moment again. "Seriously, she couldn't make it, but she can't wait to see you. She's in Atlanta at one of these fashion holding warehouses, and of course, she's on a buying frenzy for her dress store. She'll be back in a day or so. The store's doing pretty good now that she's been selling purses and those animal print thingies that go over the shoulders." He smiled.

"You mean scarves?"

"Yeah, that's it. When she started putting those in her window display with the different dresses and sequin booties people started coming in. They do look good."

"I've really missed her." She sneezed from the dust. "So, did you pop the question to her yet?" Danica smiled at the likelihood of a wedding in the near future for Josh and Jordan.

"Not yet, but I'm getting there." Josh seemed overjoyed at that prospect. "I think she'll say yes. I plan on asking her when she gets back from Atlanta."

"I hope so." Danica was grinning now, and she was genuinely happy for them both and thought they made a great couple in spite of the four-year age difference, that made no difference. Jordan did not care at all if she was a wee bit older than Josh. He didn't seem to mind either.

Danica and Jordan had their own unique likes and dislikes when it came to clothing, and they definitely had their own style of dressing.

9

Jordan would not be seen without her perfectly applied makeup, and Danica thought her own hazel eyes looked just fine with a little eyeshadow. Her light natural-look makeup from an exclusive department store seemed adequate for her clear skin, and it was barely noticeable. Most people never even noticed when she was not wearing makeup at all.

Danica wore her shoulder length, light brown hair in soft curls sometimes, but a ponytail and cap worked best for her outdoorsy lifestyle. She knew she was a little tomboyish and energetic, especially in games and sports, but everyone said she was a cute tomboy and she was definitely well mannered. Whereas, Jordan kept her dark brown hair in a more high-maintenance hairstyle with streaks, and it did look good, especially with her funky style of clothing that seemed to set it off in a great way.

Danica was certainly feminine in her own way and definitely loved clothes, but preferred her designer jeans any day over dresses, and her cargo pants were for canoeing and camping only. Even so, she was not opposed to wearing a frilly dress every now and then when her grandpa took them to something special. On more than one occasion, Danica had met some high-ranking officers at special dinners and conferences, but for today she felt good in her cargo pants, black tee-shirt with kittens, and a pink cap.

"That about does it. It's sorta kinda clean." Josh's voice again brought Danica's thoughts back to what they were doing. Almost all traces of dust were now removed from the canoe, so they moved it on down to the river's edge. Finally, they had it loaded and were ready for their long-awaited excursion down the river.

Danica Larsen was delighted to be back home and ready to relax as well as catch up on the local news. She had enlisted in the army after a couple of years in college and had been the armed guard to a chaplain in Afghanistan. As the Chaplain's guard and assistant, she provided backup to him and would do everything from managing supplies to preparing space for worship, but most of all, she was the Chaplain's bodyguard and never even saw combat. She knew that was a fortunate thing for her.

Afghanistan was still so fresh in her mind that she could still feel the usual sadness come over her when she would think back to the numerous spiritual issues that had challenged some soldiers. Some issues were obvious to Danica, but the confidential issues stayed confidential.

She immediately pushed those thoughts aside as they shoved the canoe into the edge of the murky water and away from the large two-story luxury home her grandpa took great pride in. Life had been good for Danica after going to live with her grandparents, but still, she missed her mother.

Danica stepped cautiously into the unsteady canoe first. She had to be careful to not upset or turn it over. Josh followed. He put his paddle into the shallow water and pushed it into the sand; she felt the canoe move out and away from the bank of the river and into deeper water.

"Okay, we're off." Josh laughed as they both put their paddles into the water and began to paddle with even strokes.

Right away Josh wanted to know about Alex. It struck Danica as a little humorous the way he said, "So, what are you going to do about Alex?" He said it in a low and sinister tone of voice just playing with her because he knew that Alex was still a touchy subject with her, and he wanted to keep his questions light. However, he was curious and wanted to know what was going on.

Josh intently waited for her answer as their paddles slowly sliced through the water as they continued to move the canoe further away from their grandpa's house.

"Don't know." Danica was still a little amused at Josh's tone of voice that almost sounded suspicious. "But you say that as if I have him buried in the backyard or something." Danica laughed as she tossed her ponytail like a little girl would, and then casually pointed to a softshell turtle sunning on a log near the river's bank.

"Hey, I didn't actually say that, but you must have thought about doing it, now didn't you?" Joking with her in a sly tone of voice, he said, "Come on, admit it, you did, didn't you?" He paused a moment. "Confess it, you buried him in the backyard. Now, didn't you? I know you did." Josh Anderson, twenty-seven and just out of law school was laughing now as he teased her back knowing she was more than capable of taking care of herself, but her moral code would never allow her to do something as egregious as that.

Danica noticed that he had gained a little weight since she had been gone, but he did say that he had started working out. His blond hair was a little longer too and almost covered the collar of his brand-new white sports fishing shirt that Jordan had brought back from one of her buying trips. His blue eyes seemed to look bluer next to his tanned skin.

Josh couldn't help but turn his attention to a mother duck and her baby ducklings swimming past them. "Look Danica." He nodded over to his right towards the ducks.

"Awwww, how sweet." She smiled and was genuinely pleased. "But about Alex, of course he's not buried in the backyard, he just skipped out, but I could have wrung his friggin neck for gambling my money away the way he did." Danica's face was beginning to show profound disgust because she felt a little silly for having trusted Alex. That money had been part of the insurance money her mother had left for her, and the little bit of money her grandpa had given to him. She really thought she knew better than this, to get beat out of money, that is. But why wouldn't she trust him? She had known him the better part of her life.

Anyway, now that she was back from Afghanistan, she just wanted to move forward and try to make some sense out of things, if she could. "I just thought I could trust him, that's all."

"Yeah seriously, we all did." Josh frowned a little. "Do you think you'll ever see that money again?"

"Probably not." It was simple, or should be, how Alex, their good friend, her ex-on and off boyfriend had wasted her money while she was away. She had joined the Army during an off-season with Alex, and she had to admit to herself that she had wanted the adventure of getting out of Tampa for a while. Even though her relationship with him didn't work out, she still thought at the time, that she could trust him business wise, and quite honestly, so did her grandpa. So, at twenty-six and a little confused, Danica enlisted in the Army after so incautiously investing too much money into the surf equipment shop that Alex had agreed to run, and now at thirty, she was trying to get her thoughts together and go forward with her life.

"Not good." Josh just shook his head and gently kept paddling. "Want to hear my duck call?"

"No, absolutely not! That's atrocious!" She was laughing again as they passed some well-manicured lawns that came almost to the shoreline of the river.

"Oh, come on Danica. It's not that bad."
"Yes, it is."
Each home was different in appearance, unlike a subdivision where they were all similar in appearance, and some of these along the river had their own little dock with a boat of some sort. Every now and then, there was a gazebo with pretty flowers and vines growing up the sides. Danica's most-liked gazebo was the one with the purple Mexican Petunias scattered among the pink and yellow rose bushes. Butterflies were already flitting about among the

colorful blooms of the Petunias that were threatening to invade portions of that backyard.

That morning especially, the freshness of the grass and shrubs was particularly captivating. She took a deep breath of the fresh air and basked in the dewiness of the moment. She thought for a moment that she caught a whiff of honeysuckles and that brought a smile to her face, but she reminded herself that they were evening bloomers and it was probably not even a honeysuckle at all, but another type of flower.

"So anyway, where is he now?" The sound of Josh's voice pulled her thoughts back again to the situation with Alex.

"Don't know, probably holed up in a casino somewhere. It's obvious now that he'd bet on anything. He'd probably gamble me away if he could." She laughed, but Josh heard the contempt in her voice. So now, in retrospect, Danica saw that this had become a pattern with Alex, and it probably wouldn't change. She thought it was best to put him in her past and cut her losses. "Yeah, it was just sucky, and I'll deal with it another day," she said. "I'm through with his nonsense."

Danica was beginning to feel mentally tired from it all again and glad that Josh had his back to her and couldn't see that she was on the verge of tears again. She continued to paddle, releasing some of the tension that had been building up for quite some time now. She knew she was still a mess from this situation with Alex, but for today she just wanted to rest and then she would be able to decide about her future. She thought she might go back to college; she wasn't sure.

"Did you hear that?" Danica forced a giggle and hoped to change the mood.

"Nothing but a frog croaking." Josh was quick to respond.

"Yeah, that's the male frog trying to look cute to the female, and she probably thinks his croaking is hot. I'll bet she's hoping he'll hurry up and make a move." Danica kept moving the paddle through the water as she enjoyed her surroundings and the feel of the occasional splatters of water that was like splashes of new energy, which she so badly needed. It was April and beginning to feel a little hot, but on the river the gentle and cool breezes were welcomed.

"Silly, I think frogs croak at night." Josh was happy to see that Danica was smiling again.

"Well, whatever you say." She was laughing by now.

CHAPTER 2

The stunning, bright pink wings of several roseate spoonbills feeding caught Danica's attention as she gently moved her paddle through the water taking special care to not scare the birds away. Each time the paddle cut through the water she felt the magic of the moment as she waited for the 'perfect' timing to stop and take the 'perfect' photo. The tranquility of canoeing and taking photos was like a drench of therapy that she could really use right now.

And, as if by some more special magic, the color and shape of the spoonbill's ruby-colored legs captured her complete attention pleasing her aesthetic senses beyond words. When the sun touched their backs, it set off what appeared to be silver sparkles that bounced in every direction causing her to soon forgot all about Alex. So, for the moment, all she wanted to do was take photos, go forward with her life, and without him.

They soon paused again long enough to take a couple of pictures of four egrets that seemed to strike a dramatic pose for them and then Danica and Josh were soon back on their way.

"Anyway, it's good to be back home." Danica tilted her head back and took in a deep breath of the river air. "Florida, home sweet home. What a great breeze."

"Oh yes, and get a load of that gator over there." Josh waved his tanned hand towards a large alligator that was resting on a massive limb. The limb was so low it touched the riverbank and edge of the water. Nearby, another smaller alligator was sleeping on the riverbank near a lot of lush greenery and a few scattered lily pads that were on the water's surface.

"He looks quite comfortable," Danica said, and was clearly amused. They both rested a moment from paddling and just let the canoe drift. After a few minutes, Josh gently moved his paddle through the water again to get past the sleeping alligators without disturbing them.

"Wow, it's big," Danica said almost in a whisper as they quietly passed the larger alligator.

They paddled again for a while without saying a word. Danica could feel her paddle slicing through the water on her left side as Josh focused on the right side. Danica was eyeing the bridge ahead with uncertainty dreading the thoughts of having to pass under it. "Oh yuck, I shudder every time we go under this bridge. It's so spider infested looking, and remember the time the mean kids threw the rocks at us from the top of the bridge?"

"Oh yeah, sweet memories." Josh grimaced. "What little shits! One rock just missed my head. They had nothing better to do I guess."

They went under the bridge without issues and enjoyed the next hour taking pictures of unusual sights and especially the greenery. Some foliage and plants were exuding a distinctive aroma that was somewhat citrus smelling and relaxing. Danica was not quite sure which plants had that great smell, but it was all very refreshing to her senses. The deep green foliage was a good background for some of the more colorful plants and made good choices for photos of turtles sunning on logs.

They passed more roseate spoonbills that were parading around oblivious to anything outside their own private little world. The soft way the sun was scintillating off their bright pink feathers was breathtaking and once again, Danica realized how happy she was to be back home.

After a few minutes Josh laughed and pointed. "Hey, look at the egrets!"

Her pleasure quickly turned to disgust because about that time one egret slurped down a snake to Danica's dislike. "Gross! That was just plain nasty."

"Yep." Josh snickered.

After canoeing maybe another half a mile, they soon reached a dense, narrow area of the river that had lots of snags and downed, rotted logs. They both knew what that meant, so without words and not having a choice, they both got out into the shallow, murky water, shoes and all and lifted the canoe over the obstacles. Josh was the first to go over the downed logs but not before snagging his new white shirt on a jagged branch and tearing the pocket loose. "Now wouldn't you know it. I like this shirt too."

"Not a problem, Jordan can fix it." Danica assured him.

"You're sure?"

"Absolutely!"

Without hesitation, Josh went under some drooping limbs that had moss hanging and had to push them out of the way to make way for the canoe to go through. Danica followed. As soon as they were safely on the other side of the downed logs, they were amused to see two otters playing friskily near a clump of twigs and rocks along the bank. They were too cute to disturb.

They quietly got back into the canoe and paddled on around a bend in the river where large roots were sticking out from the side of the riverbank. The meandering river had eroded sediments from the outside bend of the river and deposited them further down on the inside of the other side of the river. Individual sweeping meanders occasionally showed exposed roots.

Large branches from the huge trees hung out and draped over the water. Just in time, Danica leaned over and yelled to Josh. "Duck." He quickly lowered his head and upper body to avoid a snake that dangled from a limb.

"Oh no!" Josh had a startled look on his face. Danica looked in the direction of his intent gaze and the strong 'rotten cabbage' smell that is so distinctive of water snakes was thick in the air. Aggressive water snakes were all over the place and apparently angry at the intruders. The water to the right front of the canoe was thick with snakes writhing about and clearly agitated at being disturbed. One snake was way too close for comfort. It was coiled and ready to strike and it appeared to be on a log or something just under the water's surface. Josh knocked it away with his paddle and ordered. "Hurry, let's get outta here, they're pissed."

"Oh shit." A frightened Danica paddled faster and they didn't let up until they had put much distance between them and the snakes.

"That was godawful!" Josh shuddered.

The fear was beginning to leave them both now and Danica let out a nervous laugh. "Yeah, and let's hope we don't see another bed of snakes! That was disgusting."

"Yeah, well, at least they were non-venomous."

"I don't care! I don't like them!" Danica said.

"We have to go back that way. Whew, that was scary," Josh said. "We'll just have to stay closer to the other side of the riverbank on the way back."

"For sure," she said.

"Oh, look!" Danica pointed towards some trees to her right. "Look at the Quaker Parrots over there." They stopped to take pictures of them and soon forgot the snakes.

"No kidding, I didn't know we had wild Quaker Parrots around here," Josh said.

"Oh yes, I remember hearing that a few years back some had escaped from one of the parks. Now we have wild ones."

"Really? This is the first time I've seen them," Josh said.

"Oh, yeah, second time I've seen them."

Out of curiosity, and in search of large bass, they continued to canoe further on down the river. Eventually they went under another unpleasantly creepy bridge. It felt damp as they passed under it, and clinging vines were growing up and onto anything they could attach to, even to concrete in some places. The river had narrowed quite a bit, and thick weeds were growing up in heavy patches on both sides of the river. Branches hung out over the water and this left them only a small path to canoe through. They didn't see any other canoers and it was obvious that people rarely canoed to this isolated part of the river.

"Yikes, I think we're in the boonies." Danica laughed making light of it.

"It looks like it, but I'm getting tired." Josh complained.

"Me too. My hands hurt, my back hurts, and my butt hurts. Let's find a place to rest." She relaxed her grip on the paddle and stretched

22

her arm out straight and then flexed her wrists to try and relax her muscles. "Ouch! My legs are stiff too. I need to walk around a little bit."

"How about this place?" Josh motioned towards a clearing they finally found. It was near some ancient cypresses that had lots of gray Spanish moss hanging almost to the ground.

"Ewww, it's spooky looking, and I don't like it!" Danica pointed towards the swampy looking cypresses that were thick with moss. "And besides that, it stinks!" She wrinkled her nose at the earthy and musty odor from the algae blooms that were growing in the river.

"There's shade, and besides that, I need to rest," Josh said.

"Well, okay. It's just so swampy and we've never been this far down the river before." She looked around with a frown and then nodded. "Let's do it. I'm hungry."

"I am too."

A noisy flock of birds flew away just as Josh was stepping out of the canoe. "Here, help me with the canoe." He had come as close as he could to the river's bank and they needed to lift it out of the water.

"Gross." Danica felt slimy mud oozing into her shoes as they both carefully stepped out of the canoe, lifted it up and out of the water, and then onto the riverbank. They both had learned to bring an extra pair of shoes in their backpacks along with an extra changing of clothes. You just had to look the other way if somebody needed to change clothes. No big deal.

After stretching a little and walking around some, Danica said, "yeah, it's a little muddy here, but still not a bad place after all. Where's the lunch?"

"Try this." Josh handed Danica a sandwich from the insulated lunch bag. "It's roast beef and I smoked it myself." They didn't mind having to stand while eating and it was actually a welcomed relief from the canoe seats.

She handed Josh a hand wipe. "Do you want water or soda?"

He pointed at the water.

"Chips." She handed him a small bag of potato chips without waiting for a reply. She already knew he loved chips.

Danica took a bite of the sandwich that was on a large bun. It was thick with meat and X-hot horse radish sauce. She was not surprised at how flavorful it really was. "Whew, that's it! It's hot!" She giggled and took a long drink of her bottled water. "That's what I like!" She felt the 'straight up the nose' heat coming out of her nostrils from the heat of the horse radish. "It's good!" She was still giggling. "Did you ever wonder why it's so much fun eating something hot?"

"Yeah, like the hot jawbreakers we used to eat when we were kids," he said.

"Yeah."

"Kids love to eat hot stuff and make their mouths burn. Go figure. Anyway, I thought you'd like this." Josh laughed and took a bite. "Oh, yeah, it's hot!" He grabbed his water bottle and took a drink, but then said, "I need some soda too. Whew!"

Josh did some of the cooking when they had family cookouts, and Grandpa would make their homemade wine. It was from a recipe that had been in the family for a long time. It was actually her great, great, grandfather's recipe. Danica smirked a little because she had suspected for a long time that the 'clear as moonshine' wine was indeed the family's moonshine recipe, but nobody would say that because they didn't want to make great, great grandfather seem less than the respectable gentleman he really was. She thought about how smooth it was going down, and everybody loved it. It definitely kicked butt, and she had to suppress a giggle at this thought about her grandpa's iffy wine that was definitely high-proof.

"Did you let grandpa taste this? It's really good after it stops burning," she said.

"Oh yeah, he likes it, and I got a new smoker. You can really tell the difference in the taste of the meat."

"I noticed that. It's great," she said.

"Want another one?" Josh said motioning towards the sandwiches as he took another one for himself.

Her light brown ponytail that was neatly tucked through the back opening of her cap swung back and forth as she shook her head. "No, that was huge, but thanks anyway."

"Hey, I'm gonna fish a little," Josh said.

"Is it ok if I try out your metal detector?" Danica was already pulling it out of the canoe before Josh had a chance to answer.

"Yeah, sure. I got a new one. You can use it underwater too." He was obviously more interested in casting his line and catching the largemouth bass that always seemed to pass him by.

"Hey, get a whiff of this new bait." Josh laughed. "The guy at the bait shop said the fish love it. He said to try this along with the worms and see which one works the best. So, let's see if it works."

"Ugh, that stinks! Get it outta here." Danica covered her mouth and nose with her hand and backed away. She moved on down to another area and away from that repulsive smell.

After a few minutes and down by the river's edge, Danica motioned for Josh to 'come here'.

"Hey, get a look at this!" She was excited as she held up an object coated with dirt.

"What is it?" Josh was curious to see what she had found. "That's interesting. Here, wash it off." He offered an unopened bottle of water.

Danica cleaned it the best she could and then dried it on the black tee-shirt she was wearing. She examined it closely, but all she could tell about it was that it was very old, and a pendant of some sort.

"It's definitely a Native American artifact." She ran her fingers across the front of it and scraped some dirt off with her sports length fingernails. She thought she was feeling the imprint of a bird. She poured more water over it and then she could tell that it was indeed the imprint of a bird.

"This is exciting."

"I know. Let me see." Josh was just as curious as she was.

Danica pondered over this unique item and was curious about the native person that had lost it so long ago. "I wonder who lost it? And, the person actually stood right here, on this very spot. It's wild! I wonder what the person looked like and what they were doing."

She gently wiped it some more. "Wow! This just blows me away."

Josh leaned in even closer. "Impressive. It does make you wonder who lost it."

"I know." She zipped it up securely in one of the pockets of her camouflage cargo pants. Josh went back to fish some more. She tucked the unfinished bottle of water into another pocket and then went back to do some more metal detecting. She focused her attention on this one area in hopes she would find something else. She even checked along the edge of the river and did find something else covered in about six inches of water. She brushed at some loose sand and uncovered three stone arrowheads that were there in plain view, and they were exquisitely hand-chiseled and beautiful. She tucked them away into the same pocket that held the pendant. She was ecstatic with this spectacular find and couldn't quit thinking about who could have lost those items. Smiling, she decided that it was probably a 'he', and she tried to imagine what 'he, the brave warrior' looked like. She decided that 'he, the brave warrior' was probably quite handsome and she giggled at her own girlish imagination that had been a part of her animated personality for a long time.

About forty-five minutes later Josh yelled out. "Hey Danica, my line's tangled up on something; can you come cut it for me?" Josh stretched out the line with both hands showing her where to cut, and as soon as she did, he let the water lilies and weeds have the other end of the line and hook. It was a tangled-up mess and not worth wasting the time to untangle it. He immediately started gathering up the fishing gear and mumbled. "Thanks, no bass today." He sounded a little disappointed.

"No problem." She quickly slid her grandpa's combat knife back into its sheath.

Her heart softened again thinking about their retired Navy SEAL grandpa. She remembered the day he had given them both a combat knife and told them to never go canoeing or camping without it. His words stayed with her. "You just never know when you'll need it."

His eyes narrowed as he gave them advice. "And don't hesitate to use it. Make every thrust powerful and a kill."

"Okay." They both nodded. They knew he wasn't joking this time, and Danica also knew that he realized she was still dealing with some anxiety since the sucky day her mom had died. She had learned too young in life that heart attacks are nasty and death isn't nice. However, in looking back, she realized that the only thing that had been nice after her mother's death was living with her grandparents in a nice home on the river. She got along great with Josh, and her grandpa had taught them both to shoot his 45-caliber semi-automatic pistol, 9mm pistol, 38 Special and 22 revolvers, all handguns. However, Danica liked the revolvers the best and never tired of going to the shooting range.

Her aging grandpa had insisted that archery was also a necessity, and it was fun. It was also fun going to gun shows, and she especially loved the Native American crafts that she bought there. She had quite a collection. Danica enjoyed all of that, even going with her grandparents to church on Sundays. It was her grandparent's firm belief that you should always consider your maker.

Danica sighed remembering that her grandma would occasionally go with them to shoot the bow, but she didn't feel well a lot of the time and didn't really enjoy it there at the end. Danica felt the usual wave of sadness again remembering how her grandma had once loved to shoot her 38 Special, but no more, not since the cancer. Her grandma had been in the Navy too, anchor tattoo on the ankle and all, but she didn't stay in as long as her grandpa had. She died just six months before Danica went into the Army, and it was a sad day when they laid her to rest.

"We should head back," Danica suggested.

"I think you're right. Yeah, let's go," Josh agreed.

They quickly loaded and secured some things to the canoe and then left. Danica was more than glad to be out of the real swampy areas and back into areas that were not so overgrown with vines and bushes. They finally made their way out of the real narrow areas and then they went back under the damp bridge.

Danica laughed. "This bridge is so grotesque and creepy."

"It's not grotesque. Nothing is that bad," he said.

"Yes, it is! I can't wait to get back to civilization."

They soon reached an area of the river that was wide, and they saw other people canoeing there.

Suddenly, Danica was abruptly jolted forward with a hard jerk. A loud bang had startled them both, and a huge splash sent water spraying. The canoe dangerously rocked back and forth. She was horrified to realize that her paddle had accidentally hit an alligator in the head. She had never even seen it until out of the corner of her eye, she saw a confused alligator thrashing about and then it went under with a swoosh and capsized the canoe.

Josh and Danica both fell into the water along with the metal detector and foolishly un-worn life vests that they had carelessly used as cushions. Josh tried to reach her, but she slipped away from his grasp and the dark river took possession of her and pulled her away from him. He was helpless to pull her back up. A nearby boater noticed the confusion and managed to pull Josh to safety. He called 911 for help to find Danica.

The sheriff's department searched late into the night with K-9's and infrared cameras, and then again the next day and turned up nothing. Josh wondered how many times he would have to re-tell the story because he was just as confused as everybody else. By this time, Jordan had arrived and Josh's heart ached to see her softly shedding tears for her longtime friend that they had all loved.

The helicopter and rescue dive crews reluctantly gave up the search on Friday, April 21, 2017 after finding absolutely nothing but her cap, and Josh sadly watched as a broken old man with arthritic knees hobbled off to his pickup truck. Josh couldn't hold back the tears any longer as this once powerhouse of a man struggled to get into his pickup truck. Their grandpa slumped over the steering wheel and quietly cried.

"Grandpa!" Josh ran up to the pickup truck and reached through the opened door to give him a comforting hug. "I tried my best to reach her, but it seemed like she was fighting me. I couldn't hold on to her. She just slipped away."

"I know, don't blame yourself." Augustus (Gus) Larsen just sat there looking smaller than usual in his white V-neck tee-shirt he was accustomed to wearing these days. His 5'10" frame seemed to shrink down into the front seat of the truck he had affectionately named 'Sage Hen'. He looked small next to Josh's 6'3" frame, but in his younger days, he was an excellent swimmer and easily met the physical requirements to become a Navy SEAL. Josh knew how much Danica had loved this old man. He loved him too.

CHAPTER 3

As soon as the canoe turned over, a helpless Danica felt the long eelgrasses in the river twist and entangle her arms and legs making it impossible to swim upwards and to safety. She felt herself sinking beneath the murky, cold waters, and she slowly drifted down among the growth at the bottom of the river.

A sudden current pulled her free for a moment and swept her along the bottom of the river dragging her arm and shoulder against the side of a large rock. She was completely unaware that this rock was a fragment of the meteorite that had hit the earth on June 7, 1536 creating a curvature in gravity that did indeed make it possible for her to slip through a weak tear in space-time and go back in time to another dimension.

Danica was powerless as the current pulled her towards the meteorite and in towards a large opening, or hole that was beneath it, and in a split second the current sucked her inside the rock.

A sudden hissing sound of rushing water against rock brought Danica to the horrible realization that she was actually inside the rock when suddenly a bluish light gradually opened up the way before her. With a swoosh and with great surprise, she was moving exceedingly fast through the water and in towards this bluish light when it exploded into many shades of glowing blue radiation particles that were dust like in appearance. At warp speed, these particles started settling into layers like that of a blue rainbow. In amazement, Danica saw the first layer of the lightest blue dust particles settle downward from left to right, forming the first layer of the rainbow. Next, another layer that was a little darker settled on top of the first layer. Layer after layer settled on top of each other. Each layer was darker and more beautiful than the previous layer until a beautiful blue rainbow had formed.

Finally, and without warning, an eerie bone-chilling stillness came over her as she slipped under the blue rainbow. She didn't have a clue that because of the small curvature in gravity a fearsome thing had just taken place. She was actually going back in time through a portal to another dimension where the beautiful people lived–to the year 1624–to wilderness Florida.

After she had slipped under the blue rainbow, she felt herself slide down and out the other side of the huge rock that was a fragment of the meteorite. Danica landed in an open area of dark water surrounded by much greenery, beautiful pink flowers, and bright sunlight. She was aware of a pleasantly sweet smell and was quick to recognize it as Magnolia flowers, except the smell was strong and sharp, much like essential oils.

Immediately, she felt a confident and powerful hand on her hand pull her up and out of the water. This strong hand pulled her into a strange canoe and into an unfamiliar land, **Florida, year 1624.**

She gasped for breath as she slumped forward falling into the bottom of this impressively large and hand-carved canoe. After she had rested for a moment, she rolled over to her side and recognized odors of wood, leather, and some type of oily substance that had a musky smell. Her hand slid over the rough bottom of the canoe that was puzzling and unfamiliar, not at all like her much smaller canoe that she had shared with Josh just a short time before.

The afternoon sun was directly in her eyes, but she could still make out the image of a person sitting just above her. It was a large person, and with great skill he began paddling the canoe forward with impressive expertise and force. She held her hand up to block the sun, and oddly, he was a young, slightly tan skinned person with attractively strong and rough-hewn facial features. He had obviously pulled her into his canoe and for whatever reasons, she didn't know. In spite of his captivating face, he had an angry and deadly demeanor that terrified her. He had a serious and hard look on his face that said he could kill someone or something, and she was sure he would kill her.

In one frantic glance, her eyes moved down his body taking in every detail of his physical structure and then back up capturing every single detail about his clothing. She saw bits of fur interlaced with a red and white strip of cloth that partially covered his loose, black topknot, and from this headpiece, she saw a strip of fur that interestingly trailed down his back in a graceful show of greatness. When he moved, she saw a raccoon tail dangling down behind his right ear. He had cleverly attached it to the fur strip. She had not seen anything like this outside of history books, and this was unnerving to her, to say the least.

From where she was located in the bottom of the canoe, she could see three yellowish tan feathers at the left back of his headpiece, and they pointed downward. This simple, but dignified headpiece, was entrancing and set off a delicate looking multi colored shirt covering strong arms that moved in a persistent and deliberate way as he moved the canoe forward. A loose-fitting tunic with a sash around his waist covered the shirt. He wore matching silver armbands on each arm over his shirt. They were halfway between his shoulders and elbows, and they seemed to be a sign of his self-confidence and power. He proudly wore a round silver pendant with a beaded necklace that brought attention to the squareness of his masculine face. The silver earrings in his ears matched the pendant. He had his buckskin leggings tucked into soft leather moccasins that were laced up to his knees. They gently moved with him as he continued to guide the canoe along with energetic body movements and powerful strokes of the paddle. Danica was astonished at this person's strength as he maneuvered his canoe through a thick growth of water lilies and lily pads and then towards the other side of the river.

He turned his fierce eyes toward her and she cringed inside. To her relief, he looked away but then he turned to her again. "Where did you come from?" He spoke calmly and matter-of-factly. His perfect English surprised her and now his troubled, deep-set, black eyes

36

followed her every move, frightening her even more. She was increasingly sure he was going to kill her–or worse, but for now, she wished he would quit looking at her. She tried to answer him, but words wouldn't come. Now trapped like a small and frightened animal in the bottom of this rough canoe, she felt a sudden rush of uncontrollable fear and wished again that he would take his unwanted gaze off her.

When the canoe approached an area with a clearing, this person that was so unlike her silently guided the canoe to the bank of the river. As they approached the river bank he turned slightly, and when he did his leather moccasin brushed up against her face and terror surged through her. *He touched me* her thoughts screamed. She jerked back and huddled close to the side of the canoe but there was nowhere to go. Her heart raced and her thoughts were still screaming, *now, he's going to kill me.* The smell of leather from his moccasin was sharp and strong to her senses as she anticipated his next move. Nausea threatened and dread filled her. She didn't know where her strength came from, but without waiting to see what, or if this person was about to do something, she jumped up and out of the canoe. She ran until she could run no more.

Just how far she ran, she didn't know. Her rubbery knees couldn't hold her up any longer, and she was suddenly feeling dizzy. She could feel herself slipping into unconsciousness and slowly going down towards the ground where she welcomed an exhausted sleep.

She never even felt herself hit the ground and must have passed out or slept there because heavy drops of rain hitting the side of her face woke her. Terror filled her as she remembered the events of the last few hours. Silent tears slid down her cheeks and in a barely audible voice, she said, "What just happened?" She felt despair closing in and knew that only the trees and rain could hear her. "And, where am I?"

She jumped up and looked around in panic fighting the strong urge to call out for Josh. "This sucks. It just sucks." She moved her mouth but almost no sound came out. She looked in every direction hoping to see Josh but saw no one, only a path through some thick woods that she didn't recognize. She remembered the savagery of that strange man's whole demeanor and recalling the anger in his eyes struck terror in her again. She ran again until she was sure he was nowhere around.

She soon found shelter under a huge oak and dropped to the ground again in exhaustion and helplessness. Her clothes were still damp from the river, and this chilled her to the bone. Danica was beginning to feel a familiar numbness envelop her, and the extreme physical and mental fatigue was just too much for her. She had no clue how long she sat there, but it was beginning to get dark, and she was even more terrified. She let out a cynical laugh just remembering how Alex had upset her so much and now realized that it was nothing compared to this.

She remembered her cell phone and frantically unzipped her pocket. "Great, no service! Now what? And where in the hell is Josh?" She wanted to scream but feared the young man would hear her and find her.

With darkness closing in, she knew she would rather just sit here, under this tree and wait out the night than to go down that dark path ahead. She saw nothing but thick woods around her and then she heard a sinister hiss. After looking around, she saw nothing, and then more eerie sounds permeated the evening air. She recognized these sounds as Bobcats screaming and snarling at each other. She shook with terror and then noticed a low hanging limb that was a lot like the one she had climbed as a kid. Without hesitation, she climbed the tree to a fairly comfortable place to rest and then waited for morning. She knew she would not have a chance if she tried to make it through the night out in the open and she was not about to find out.

It was a long and uncomfortable night. The chilling noises she heard throughout the night stimulated her imagination almost to the point of hysteria. The hissing, the unnerving shadows cast by the moon that were coming through the trees, a screeching owl, and the crunching of twigs by 'God only knows what' added to her feelings of being totally alone.

The next morning, and after a short rain had slacked off to a misty drizzle, she climbed down out of the tree and set out in search of civilization. She hoped to find anything or anybody but the frightening young man she had first encountered. She shivered from the unknown, and her wet clothes were clinging to her body causing a chill to go over her as she quickly moved on down the thoroughly soaked path. Danica had no idea what she was doing here except she knew she would rather be back in Afghanistan than here. At least, in Afghanistan, she knew where she was as the guard to the chaplain. It was uneventful and not bad.

The path quickly turned into something out of her worst nightmare and it was creepy with thick woods and vines growing everywhere. *This sucks. This really sucks*, her frenzied thoughts just wouldn't quiet down, nor would her agonizing fear subside during her long walk through the gloomy trees. She reasoned to herself that if she could just make it through these dense woods, then surely people and activity had to be close by. Going back in the other direction towards the river and that angry man was simply not an option.

After she came out of the thick woods, she dismally looked around and all she saw was a boggy swamp with marshy areas too wet to walk on. A waterlogged path ran alongside thick bushes and trees with some small, scattered palm trees. The path headed towards what looked like another dense forest ahead. The rough path was nothing more than long deep tracks pressed into the dirt by repeated passage over time. Her disappointment was almost too much to bear, but in spite of it, she moved forward and carefully stepped around the waterlogged areas and over mud puddles in the path. She tried her cell phone again and nothing. She was afraid to go forward, but more afraid to go back.

The fast chirping from crickets was annoying to say the least. They were everywhere, supposedly nocturnal but not always, and surely not today. She heard a rustling that turned out to be a small ground rattler, and then a loud shriek cut through these other noises startling her. She shuddered and wondered if it was a fox or something. She also wondered if she had made the wrong choice in coming in this direction, but she still wouldn't turn back. She was certain she would find some signs of human life soon. Hopefully, she would find Josh. Danica realized that she needed to still her chaotic thoughts, but it didn't happen.

Another reptile slithered past her, but she continued going forward. She was used to noises from dense woods because of her love for canoeing, but this was ridiculous. It was a dangerous wilderness with no apparent way out. She knew her chaotic thoughts were getting out of control but she didn't know how to still them. She stopped for a moment to catch her breath and to try to calm this irrationality, but it didn't work. She felt her heart beating fast and she realized that the loud, gasping noise she heard was actually from her own laborious breathing. She was on the verge of hysteria and she knew it.

Shortly down the path, there were towering pine trees that moved back and forth in the wind making music and then seemed to whisper to her, *come this way*, enchanting her and luring her into a land of the unknown. Danica looked up towards the tops of the pines and felt dizzy as if she was swaying with them. She stopped walking, continued to look up and turned a half circle, then again, and again until she almost felt drunk. She became so enthralled by the psithurism, or sound coming from high in the pines that some of the fear left her, but only for the moment. Out of nowhere came a black flash racing across the path in front of her. Startled, she let out a nervous, but half-relieved laugh because she had seen many little brownish-black, feral pigs before. She also knew she had to avoid their dangerous looking tusks.

Finally, she saw a clearing with beautiful green grass that looked like a pasture for cattle, but it was void of anything that even resembled a cow. There were no people around either, so she surmised that it definitely was not somebody's farm land. Over to one side of the grass field were beautiful huge oaks with drooping limbs that invited her to climb them. On the other side of the field were azalea bushes that reached at least ten feet in height and they were scattered among and under trees near the edge of some thicker woods. It was incredibly peaceful there and this calmed her a little. She was also very tired and knew she needed shelter for that night because it was looking doubtful that she would find Josh today, and she felt some comfort believing that Josh was looking for her. *This is it,* she thought. *And look at the fig trees near the stream.*

She scoped out the perfect old oak to build a temporary shelter and resting place for that night. Something that was high above the ground and away from any roaming animals or that scary young man. It just seemed like the rational thing to do and maybe her thoughts would calm down enough for her to think things through tomorrow.

While she was out looking for sturdy limbs to cut, she found several banana trees tucked in between some larger trees. They were near the stream, and they were ripe and waiting for her to come cut them loose with her grandpa's combat knife. She didn't hesitate to eat two right then and there on the spot and couldn't believe how tasty and sweet they were.

Her grandpa's combat knife came in handy again for cutting palmetto leaves. They made an excellent, temporary roof and then she found some type of larger leaves that she layered to make a cushiony seat. But first, she checked the fronts and backs of each leave for bugs or spiders. *Nothing, you can't be too sure,* she thought, turning the leaves this way and that way before placing them close together to make the temporary roof and seat. This did offer a little comfort for the time being until she could make sense out of what was happening.

She managed to get some sleep that night and set out the next morning in hopes of finding some way out. She didn't get very far and became discouraged because of the entangled vines and bushes. She realized that there was just no way out if she went in this direction, so she turned back towards the grassy area where she had spent the previous night. She spent another night there, and then another and by now her anxiety and fear was being replaced with feelings of sadness, hopelessness and depression. *I'm trapped here, and what in the hell happened,* these frequent thoughts troubled her and demanded an answer, but she just didn't have it. None of this made any sense at all. Anyway, she decided that this would just have to be her home until she could figure out what to do. She wondered what her grandpa would do in this situation, but she didn't know. What she did know was that he wouldn't cry about it, and he would find a solution. Realizing this, a calmness came over her and she thought, *there is a way and I'll find it.* She didn't know how, but she knew she would.

It was certainly the rainy season and Danica soon started wondering if it would ever quit raining, so each day she added to her temporary shelter by layering palmetto leaves for a roof in such a way as to provide a decent shelter. The palmetto leaves were layered in rows and rows over vines that she had cut and wrapped around thick limbs, and then she tied each one in place with flexible vines. She also let the palmetto leaves extend on down the sides for added protection from bad weather. She then took more of the smaller vines and painstakingly tied them around thick branches and made the most exotic hammock of all time. It extended out a little over the stream and she felt a serious adrenaline rush each time she got into it. She made it oversized to keep her from taking a disastrous fall when she went to sleep in it. She secured everything together one last time and dared it to come loose. It took a lot of work and time, but well worth it.

Danica still had no clue where she was or where to go, so she just stayed there in the trees for the time being. She wanted to go home, but for now she knew she had to accept these trees as her home if she wanted to survive. Her preferred trees were beneath a canopy of larger trees and vines, and as the days passed, she wondered if she would ever see her grandpa, Josh and Jordan again. She also wondered if they were looking for her. At first, she thought so, but now she wondered if they had given up their search for her. She hoped they were still looking, but had no way of knowing that they had already presumed she was dead.

Resting high in the old oak with gigantic limbs, she felt fairly safe in her tree shelter. It was roughly made, but offered some comfort and relief from the hot sun and occasional rain. She had also cleverly used large leaves to catch rainwater to drink and to fill her water bottle for later use. She eventually decided it was safe to drink from the stream below, and that it was free from harmful algal bloom bacteria.

Large branches that swooped downward and touched the ground in some places made it easy to climb to good resting places on these huge limbs. Now moderately comfortable, Danica could only imagine what the mockingbirds were singing about as she speculatively looked around from her new temporary home in the huge oaks that protected her from wild animals and slithering things. And there were truly some fierce animals, as well as cute animals, but the most dreaded thing was the brown recluse spiders that favored rotting tree bark and the insides of dark tree stumps. In one certain rotted tree stump, she saw at least a hundred or more spiders, so she went nowhere near that tree. They were huge and she knew the venom could make her seriously ill if she was bitten by one.

When she had at first noticed the spiders, she was down by the stream trying to fish with not much luck. Her pole was so crude she had to laugh at it. Her line was a thin piece of vine, and then for the hook - well, there was the real problem. There was absolutely nothing worthy of using for a hook. It just looked silly so she abandoned that thought for the time being, but while she was just lingering there, she realized that she was almost upon an infestation of spiders that sent her scurrying to a safer place.

She decided that the safer place was surely her tree shelter and after climbing back to the shelter, she deliberately focused on the stunning views of the scattered Yellow Jasmine vines to get her mind off the spiders. The Yellow Jasmines attracted phenomenal butterflies that were a far cry better looking than the spiders, and it was even more peaceful watching their wings flutter and take them into one direction and then without any rhyme or reason they would fly in another direction. After getting into a comfortable position in her hammock, she relaxed and all of this peacefulness lulled her into a sleepy warmth. Perched high above many of the other trees and bushes, but still under the canopy of even larger trees, nothing was worrying her at the moment – and she had all but forgotten the spiders. She felt fairly relaxed and drifted off into a peaceful sleep.

Movement woke her from a sound sleep. She raised her head slightly and made a scrunched-up face; narrowing her eyes, she looked around to something somewhat spectacular and comical. Raising her voice, she gave an authoritative order. "Okay! Go on, get outta here. Now I have a monkey's ass in my face!" With her hand, she shooed the curious monkey back and away towards another limb.

After a few minutes, the monkey was back and wanted to snuggle up against Danica. "Aww, come on now, you might have fleas. Go on, get away." When the monkey turned to the side, Danica noticed a small chain on her neck. "Hey girl, where did this come from?" She touched the chain to get a closer look. "Wow, I'll bet that hurts, doesn't it?"

The monkey seemed to know what Danica was talking about and became very still so Danica could examine the chain that was too tight around her neck.

"Good girl, stay still and I'll see what I can do to get this off." She used her grandpa's knife to pry the chain loose. It was off in a few minutes and the monkey seemed relieved.

Danica stroked her a time or two and welcomed the company of the monkey to talk to. "So, it looks like you are as lost as I am."

The monkey tried to snuggle even closer.

"How did you get here?" Danica could only wonder. Nothing made any sense at all. "But hey, you're company, so stay awhile. It seems like you're as lonely as I am."

It was obvious to Danica that the monkey had been used to cuddling when she was with her previous owner, whoever that was.

Danica reached over and got one of the bananas. "And I'll bet you want one of these, now don't you. Okay, I'll share."

CHAPTER 4

After dining on the large, wild figs and bananas for three days, she set out in search of cattails to eat and to use on the nasty scratches she still had from the accident. She thought she would put one on the monkey's neck too because she had noticed that the chain had left a deep, red mark.

She found some cattails, but they were in hard-to-reach marshy areas. However, they were not entirely impossible to get to. She had once read about the medicinal qualities of cattails and how they had many uses because of their absorbency, and plus that, they were also edible if roasted.   The book had also mentioned chew sticks made out of twigs for teeth cleaning. So, she thought it would be a good idea to get some of those too. She decided that the fig tree would provide some good chew sticks for now. She had heard that the taste was not bad and if you chew one end down until it frayed, you could then brush it against your teeth until the gums feel tingly and clean. Oak bark was definitely on her mental list to also try.

Thinking of roasted cattails, she remembered to check her lighter to see if it still worked. It did. She checked the other pockets of her cargo pants and her compass was still in good shape. In another pocket, her nail clippers were still there and then her hand touched the forgotten pendant. Mildly interested, she looked at it again and then put it back into her pocket.

She decided to go for the only two cattails that were within reach because low-growing shrubs surrounded them, and the area was heavy with water. Where she was standing, the ground was unusually soft and mushy, so Danica settled for the two cattails and then decided to get out of there. It just seemed too unsafe to stand there with no firm footing, and besides that she didn't want any encounters with water moccasins, aka cottonmouths. She knew they usually would not attack unless they felt threatened, but even so, she decided to get out of their habitat and let them have it all to themselves.

Later, she cut an end off one cattail, and then cut it open to wrap around the ugly scratch on her ankle that was still looking pretty nasty. About that time the monkey came back and was curious about what Danica was doing. "Here girl, be still and let me put this on you, you'll feel better." She took a piece of cattail and placed it on the monkey's neck where the chain had left the red marks and then the monkey got as close as possible to her. "You are a snuggler. Now, aren't you?" The monkey's cute behavior was causing Danica to grow fonder of her each day and she lovingly stroked her back and head.

She saved the rest of the cattail for later use because of their nutritive values. When she did roast it, she quickly spit it out while making a face and thinking, *it tastes like shit.* Luckily for her, she had the chew sticks she had cut from the fig trees and that got the taste out of her mouth.

The trees were gradually becoming her safe haven, and her despair was beginning to fade. For her own mental well-being she would deliberately amuse herself by trying to imitate the many songs of the mockingbirds. Watching the birds was something to occupy her time. And it was interesting to see them fly from tree to tree completely incognizant of their observer. She thought back to the time she had observed the baby mockingbirds from her upstairs bedroom window as each baby bird, one at a time, would try their wings to fly. They were all soon proficient at it, and now, here in the trees, the mockingbird trill in the mornings soothed her and made her feel somewhat at peace with the world she was now coming to know as her temporary home. However, she missed her grandpa, Josh and Jordan every day and never stopped looking for them.

Danica also used her grandpa's knife to cut a piece of wood to make a small, wide tooth comb. She used the point of the knife to cut the teeth perfectly straight and in line with the grain. She rounded the top edges and tried her hand at ornate woodcarving along the top of the comb. She thought it looked weird but it got the tangles out of her hair.

She still had no clue where to go or what to do, so she decided to stay in the trees for a while longer, and almost daily she would walk down to a beautiful and serene beach she had discovered while out looking for food. She found huge clams and roasted them over a fire that she had no trouble starting. The clams were fairly easy to get to, but she had to avoid jellyfish that surrounded them, and in no way did she want to deal with their sting that could leave blisters.

Every day the monkey came back to check her out and to play. Danica named her Rose Marie because she had such an endearing face, and it was amusing the way she seemed to try to communicate with her. They quickly became best buddies and Danica would soothingly talk to her. "You just want me to play with you. Now, don't you? And I suspect this was your tree long before I came along, wasn't it?" The monkey listened intently as if she understood every word. "How would you like it if I made you a comb? You'd probably like that, wouldn't you? I'll see what I can do tomorrow."

The next day, she did just that. She made a special comb just for Rose Marie. It had wide teeth and she was sure it would work. When she climbed back up into the tree, Rose Marie was there and waiting for her. "Here, let's see how you like this?" Danica gently combed Rose Marie's hair until the monkey shut her eyes and almost went to sleep. "I do believe you were a girl's monkey in your other life. I just wonder where you came from and how you got here, but you probably wonder that about me too. Don't you."

Danica would climb limbs to higher places to observe the area, and especially to always be on the look-out for Josh. *No such luck though*, she thought, and she soon noticed that Rose Marie would follow her. She would then jump to other limbs that were sturdy enough to hold her weight just to see if the monkey would follow. She did. All Danica would have to say was, "Come on girl," and the monkey would follow her almost anywhere and in the evenings the monkey would snuggle up close to her. It sure beat the sadness of being socially isolated.

Danica could tell that she was becoming muscular and strong beneath her clothes that were quickly wearing out. Her legs and arms got plenty of a workout climbing the trees and running through the nearby woods. Also, her grip and wrists were becoming more powerful than she would have ever imagined possible.

One day, while she was out walking, she conveniently discovered a patch of what looked like aloe vera. This was puzzling because it was a lot larger than the plants she was used to seeing. Upon closer inspection, she was certain that it was indeed aloe vera. She cut a few pieces to use for cosmetic purposes. She especially wanted it for her face and hands and thought it might suffice as shampoo and soap to retain moisture. *It's worth a try*, she thought.

She soon discovered a cave that was complete with bats. The cave came in handy during a recent thunderstorm that had lightening striking extremely close to the trees where she stayed, and it protected her from a strong wind that chilled her to the bone.

"Gross!" she said out loud when she went inside the cave and got a whiff of bat urine and excrement. She thought it smelled a little like an old rabbit cage that had not been cleaned in - forever! "Oh, gag me," she said out loud and covered her mouth and nose with her hand as she slowly made her way deeper inside the cave. It was really scary, but it was still better than the electrical storm taking place outside the cave. She carefully inched along until she finally found a spot where she could just sit without having to dodge bat dung. The bats conveniently stayed near the opening of the cave, so she stayed out of their way and in that one spot until the storm was over. She didn't want to disturb the sleeping bats that were hanging from the cave ceiling, if she did, she knew they would probably fly around chaotically and crash into her, *because that's just what they do*, she thought.

After the storm was over, she went back to the trees and to her friend, the monkey. Rose Marie would have no part of the cave, so she had to be on her own during the thunderstorm. Anyway, when there was no severe weather, Danica preferred the trees over the bats any day. When she went back to the tree shelter, she was pleased to find that Rose Marie was still there and safe.

"Girl, I'm so glad you're safe." Danica soothingly stroked the monkey's back a few times. "But of course, you would be safe, you're a monkey and can take care of yourself. Right?" she said smiling. "But, where did you go or hide? You must have a secret hiding place under some rock crevice, or hollow log or something. Right?"

The monkey looked at her as if she understood her every word, but Danica was sure she just wanted to be petted. She stroked Rose Marie's back a few more times and all was well again.

One of the huge limbs spread way out over a part of the stream where she would bathe and swim daily, now that she had determined the water was safe to drink and swim in. She would often just hang out on the limb directly over the stream and throw pebbles just to watch the concentric circles go out.

At any given time throughout the day, she would watch to see which animals would come up for a drink. She soon noticed which of the animals lived in perfect harmony together and which did not. She watched a female deer - or doe, just leisurely walking around, and then she stopped, turned and looked straight at Danica. *She's beautiful,* Danica thought as she carefully studied every last detail of the deer. She was light brown and could have easily weighed 150 pounds. She stood gracefully still for the longest time as if posing for a photo shoot, and then she gracefully moved on back into the woods. *I sure wish I had my camera,* Danica thought.

It was equally as interesting to see how the gray fox would forage for food and stalk wild roosters that seemed to roam freely. The fox had a habit of killing several at a time by taking their heads off, but he would only take one to eat. Danica saw this as peculiarly gross, but for her it was a meal for that day and to her it was called survival.

Rose Marie was good company, and Danica also saw that she was of great value to her if a dangerous animal came near. She found that out one day when Rose Marie became panicked about something and was franticly smacking her lips, jumping up and down and making screeching noises.

"Hey, what's up girl?" Danica held her hands out as if questioning her. Rose Marie had run up higher into the tree and was now looking down. "Oh no!" Danica stared down into the threatening greenish eyes of an unpredictable Puma, sometimes called a (melanistic) black Panther. Danica could feel her heart beating faster as the Puma stared at her contemplating his next move. He took a few steps in her direction and then soon lost interest and made his decision to walk away. "Whew, thanks girl for warning me."

The same thing happened the day a Red-tailed hawk, a bird of prey, was flying too close to Rose Marie. She had run lower in the tree and looked up. Danica soon learned what Rose Marie's signals meant, and she learned from her to pay attention when little twigs would break, or any unusual movement or sound. She was developing an unusually keen sense of hearing and smell which was excellent at detecting danger and the different animals had different smells making it convenient for her to know which animal was in her close proximity. Oh, the beauty of the tarsal gland, some animal pee just has a stronger and more unique scent that other animals can recognize.

Danica especially learned to love the twilight before the fall of night and learned which of the animals were nocturnal and which were not. The owl seemed to be a little bit of both.

At night she would watch a myriad of stars and hope to see a falling star so she could make a wish. Danica smiled at this because she wished that she could 'wish upon a star' and go home.

It was becoming the daily routine to go down to the beach in the early morning just to check out the area and to crab or scallop. Seafood was plentiful and tasty. One day she decided to venture farther on down the beach and the breeze was a little stronger than usual causing breaking waves in the surf zone to leave foamy bubbles. She walked along the water's edge letting the sea foam wash up around her ankles for as long as she could, and then came to many huge rocks that were blocking the way. She went around them and through some grass that had sabal palms and thickets. Finally, she was able to get back to the water's edge and the splendid sea foam that felt so good to her bare feet.

She was curious, so she walked a long way until the beach ran out and there was nothing but more palmettos, bushes, and thickets. She stooped to put her shoes back on and when she did, out of the corner of her eye she noticed a fin coming in pretty close to the shoreline. It was definitely a shark fin, and a large one. She recalled that if it's a shark, the fin cuts slowly through the water, not rising up or down, buy stays above the water in a straight line; whereas a dolphin will pop up and down quickly in one spot. So, Danica was sure this was definitely a shark. A shudder went over her and she made a mental note to stay clear of the deeper water as she made her way through the bushes.

It was difficult to get through this barrier of bushes, but she managed to find a way. About eighteen feet back from the water's edge were some extremely tall palms, and once she made her way to these, she was able to get through. There was a grassy area with sandy spots that had lots of sand spurs, or also known as burrs; she was careful to step over those little, but painful to remove stickers. A rabbit taking refuge in another thicket ran away as she came near. She made her way through those areas and came back out to a wide-open stretch of beautiful beach with foamy waves rolling in. Every now and then, the strong breeze would send little salty bursting bubbles of sea spray into her face and hair cooling her skin where the hot sun had warmed her face. She smiled and thought, *oh no, not another freckle.*

The smell of the salt water was fresh and clean, certainly something she had never experienced before. She also noticed there were no repugnant smells of diesel fuel, beer, or decaying fish so she rolled her pants legs up and took her shoes off again. She just stood there for a few minutes breathing in the clean, salty air.

Danica walked slowly along the beach enjoying the amazing breeze and admiring the way the water reflected the blue of the morning sky.

The waves along this stretch of beach were washing small amounts of seaweed up around her bare feet, and the refreshing sprays from the water were cooling. However, she had noticed that her shoes were wearing thin, but she decided that she wouldn't worry about it just yet.

She heard the loud and noisy meowing sounds from the seagulls as they demanded a handout that didn't come. Many swooped down with fluttering wings that completely surrounded her and then just as quickly, some flew away into the blinding sun. The others soon moved on down the beach.

Danica waded in the shallow water, splashing it every chance she got and pretended that the seagulls were telling her 'The Story' again. It was 'The Story' that she would tell to her grandpa over and over again when she first came to live with him and grandma. Danica held her arms out like wings, just like she did when she was a kid and pretended to be a seagull swooping in as she repeated 'The Story'.

The shimmering sunlight casually sparkles along the bay

As the soft summer breeze seems to gently say
It is time; it is time, for the seagulls to do their dance
It is time; it is time, as they take their proper stance
So regal - So sure - So exciting to see
But all too soon it's over as they fly away to sea.
Grandpa would smile and say, "and you're sure the seagulls are telling you this?"

"Yes grandpa, I'm sure," she would say.

Anyway, grandpa liked 'The Story', and she remembered the way his blue eyes would light up when she told it to him. She sighed missing him. Reluctantly she looked around at her new surroundings and couldn't help but wonder what was to become of her.

Shells were everywhere and she picked up a few of the more interesting ones. Dozens of starfish were also scattered around as if someone had placed them there to dry. Farther on down the beach Danica heard voices, feminine voices, and she just had to do it–she had to keep walking to satisfy her curiosity. She walked towards the friendly voices, and soon she was in the midst of the friendly people. They were beautiful people and she felt safe. Some were practically naked except for little flaps in the front and back of their lower bodies. The flaps were made out of moss or parts of palmetto leaves woven into coverings over cord and tied at the waist. Most were barefooted; some were caring for children, and others were preparing food. A deep basket filled to the brim with oysters was soon going to be smoked over a very cleverly made open pit. The smiling people brought her into the midst of them and offered her food and a place to rest before the evening festivities.

To her surprise, she realized that a few could speak some English. A friendly young man who had been carving out a canoe stopped what he was doing, motioned towards the gash on her ankle, and then said to her, "You come". He then ushered her past three other young men dragging their canoes out of the water. She was amazed to see that they had made all of their tools out of seashells. She walked with him for what seemed like forever and towards a small hut on stilts. "You enter now, rest," he said when they walked up some rough steps that had been chopped out of wood; obviously by using heavy blows from some sort of primitive tool.

An older woman was friendly and brought her into her hut to offer a place to rest. The old woman had a shell through her nose and deep wrinkles in her face. Danica made it a point to 'not look' at the shell or the wrinkles. Immediately, the smell of different herbs and plants were strong in the air and she knew the old woman must be a healer.

Over in the corner were two young women huddled together, and they both had their hair cut short. The short hair was apparently a sign that they were in mourning. Danica didn't even try to ask about it. It was obvious. Another young girl with short hair was sitting on a mat nearby and crying. Danica could hear the heart wrenching sobs coming from her and knew there was nothing she could do to console her.

The old woman graciously offered Danica something to eat. "You eat now." After she had eaten what tasted like smoked fish and oysters, the old woman looked at the gash Danica still had on her ankle from before and saw that it was getting red and nasty. The old woman put a soothing paste on her wound that smelled a little like sage and something else indistinguishable. She gently rubbed some on the wound and said, "You rest now." She then moved back over to the girl on the mat and gave her a few sips of a liquid that she had in a small jar like container. The sobbing soon stopped and the girl slept for a while.

Danica was grateful and rested on the soft mat the old woman had offered to her. It was near the back of the hut close to the sleeping girl.

Late that evening she smelled a different type of meat cooking. All types of fruit and vegetables were available in colorful pottery dishes and baskets that were served by women with huge muscular thighs and arms that were as large as the men's arms.

There was entertainment that night around the fire where some warriors wore cleverly painted masks with hinged jaws and danced around the fires showing off their skills and shell jewelry. Male singers came out singing in perfect unison, and gracefully the women followed with dancing, keeping perfect timing to the music of flutes and gourd rattles. The beauty of it was breathtaking to Danica and when invited to join the festivities, she didn't resist. After the dancing, there was a celebration with different types of vegetables, fruit, fish, lizards, deer and roasted hogs. She skipped the lizard and hoped no one noticed.

Other warriors with ferociously painted faces impressively walked about the edges of the village with spears and bows they had cleverly made. Every one of these warriors was well over 6'5" and well-built with tattoos on their huge thighs and arms; some carried poles with flames.

Later that night, there was a religious ceremony with the shaman contacting certain deities to gain spiritual guidance and direction. He stood strong and proud with a blue cloth over his left shoulder, and his right shoulder was bare, muscular and tattooed. They believed that the color blue would bring peace and keep bad spirits away. He wore a white, skirt-like garment under this blue cloth and had bare legs with multiple tattoos. A white fox tail elegantly dangled down from the left side of his shoulder and was attached to the blue cloth. A brownish red feather of considerable size spread out from the very center of a top knot at the top of his head. The sides of his head were shaved and he wore a stunning, golden headband with ornate designs of blue and red. The central focus of the headband was a large round stone that appeared to be a sparkling emerald. A breathtaking medallion hung in a regal way from his neck as if to signify his importance. His ears had many piercings and gold jewelry dangled from the top of his ears to the earlobes. The gems in his earrings sparkled as he moved about, and Danica was in awe of his magnificence.

After joining into the earlier festivities, with the dances and singing, Danica retreated to the sidelines and just sit there enjoying being a part of this spectacular event. She watched intently, and with astonishment at this extraordinary celebration and the impressive inhabitants of this swampland. Danica wondered where she was and if she was capable of adapting to this wilderness the way these resilient and beautiful people had.

The following morning, voices outside the healer's hut caught Danica's attention. A few minutes later, the young man entered the hut again to fetch her, and she oddly felt no fear of him.

Motioning to Danica, the young man said, "You come" and he took her to the center of the village where a meeting room was located. It was raised up higher than the other huts on a small hill that was made out of oyster shells, dirt, and other items that she couldn't quite identify. They climbed some skillfully made steps that became wider at the entrance porch; from there they went into a hall with a thatched roof and up some more steps. The actual meeting room stood even higher on a mound, and to Danica's amazement, it could possibly accommodate at least 1,000 people. It was huge.

There the war captain, shaman, and a visiting Lord were waiting. Danica's first impression of the war captain was that he was unfriendly, bad-tempered and a first-rate butthole.

Soon the chief entered and his presence was impressive. He was broad-shouldered and well built, not as tall as the others were, and he was pleasingly graceful and stylish in appearance and in mannerisms. His headdress was of many stunning feathers with a broad gold band. He wore rows of bone and shell beads around his neck with a gold pendant that had intricate circular designs drawing attention to his bare chest covered with tattoos. Brightly dyed beads of different colors dangled around a band he wore across his shoulder showing off his huge and muscular arms. He had a covering around his waist that had a long piece of brilliant red fabric coming down and covering the front of his body. At the bottom of his waistband, he had golden beads that made a popping sound when he moved or walked. His bare, muscular thighs had designs painted on with black and red paint; his face also had a large black line just under his right eye with smaller lines going down to his chin. Likewise, his arms had painted designs resembling a bird that was probably an indication of religious connections. He had an elegant, but fierce demeanor, yet he still displayed a natural courtesy towards Danica and did genuinely seem to want to help her.

At the council, they heard Danica's perplexing story about the blue rainbow and they all realized that she did not yet know the meaning of what had happened to her. She didn't realize that there had been many before her that had come to them for answers about how they could return to their home.

The chief finally spoke. "We can't help you here. There is only one that can help you to understand your predicament and that's the one that is called the lady from the stars. She has a name but it's unknown to us; they all just call her 'the lady'. She is a great distance away and you would have to go through much danger to reach her."

Everyone but the war captain agreed that she should seek her help. "You will not make it through the swamp and then the forest. There are many dangerous animals." The war captain was moving about as they continued their animated conversation.

He turned to the chief and said in a matter-of-fact way. "And she will not survive Chua and his warriors!" He turned back to Danica and said firmly and in a not very friendly manner. "I insist that you cannot go. You do not know what Chua and his warriors will do to you. They are loathsome and inflict much evil to everyone they encounter. They are hated by all and will kill you." He knew that most people in her situation did not make it through the swamp or forest and only the strongest and smartest survived.

"I have to try. I want to go home." Danica was feeling disheartened by his words.

After more conversation, they agreed that she could not make the trip alone and must have at least one guide to assist her, preferably two, or three.

"Okay, it is your choice." The chief was the one to finally speak up and offer a solution. He advised her to go back to the river, cross over it, and go down the other side of the river to a settlement where she could possibly find a guide that might be willing to take her to the lady from the stars.

"The guide that you should ask for is Elkanah Hawkins. See if he will assist you to his mother's village and from there, they will help you through the densest areas of the forest. This is your only chance." The chief turned to leave the room, then stopped and turned back to look directly into Danica's eyes. She cringed under the gaze from his fierce black eyes. "Do not attempt to go alone," the chief said and then quietly left the meeting area.

Before Danica left the village, the old woman brought her a pair of moccasins that laced up to her knees. She also offered her a soft top with long sleeves that Danica received with gratitude and did not hesitate to slip it on over her tee-shirt. She neatly tucked it in under her belt and knife. It was a perfect fit and made of a beautiful light brown fabric with blue, yellow, and red designs. Danica had feelings of gratitude because of the way the old woman had noticed her need for covering. She remembered how breezy it had become just two days ago as a firm breeze had whipped through the trees before a rain. She had become particularly cold and shivering in her thin tee-shirt.

Before she left, the old woman combed coconut water through her hair with a cleverly made comb. It was from a backbone of a large fish and then the old woman pulled her hair up and into a top knot at the top of her head. She then adorned it with dazzling white feathers and multi-colored beads that matched the colors in her top. She placed small silver bracelets on both Danica's wrists and small silver earrings in each ear. She stood back and looked at Danica. "Better," the old woman said.

"Better." Danica agreed and smiled.

The old woman picked up the nearby bowl and placed something on her wound again. It was soothing so Danica didn't question it and thanked her for all of her kindness towards her.

She set out to go back down the beach, and a short distance down were many palm trees with coconuts and several young boys gathering them. The smiling children eagerly ran over to Danica and offered her a coconut.

"Thank you." She smiled and graciously accepted the coconut.

She watched as another boy smoothly climbed a tall tree and then slowly moved back down after throwing some coconuts to the ground.

"*Alrighty, here is my hair conditioner.*" Danica thought and then waved goodbye. "I'll see you again."

The children waved until she was out of sight and some followed for a little distance, not wanting her to leave.

It was easy to back track and go back down the beach, past the mangroves and then back to the trees to rest. She wanted to say goodbye to Rose Marie because she didn't know if she would ever see her again.

"I brought you a little treat my friend." Rose Marie trustingly took the piece of coconut she offered and then Danica relaxed for the evening.

CHAPTER 5

The next morning Danica left the trees and headed out towards the river and dreaded going back through the thick woods again that was loaded with mosquitoes. It was uncomfortable, but she had no other choice if she wanted to get back home. At least most of the heavy raining had passed, and the previously soggy paths were almost dried out. She reluctantly headed back down these paths again that would take her back down the most dreaded path of all, the area she was now referring to as the 'hell path' just on the other side of the tall pines, and back to the river.

It was in the 'hell path' area where a big boar hog rain out and scared the living daylights out of her. It ran like a flash of lightening and then grunted and squealed, turned and ran in another direction. It was scary and Danica didn't know what to expect so she waited a few minutes to make sure he was gone before proceeding along the path. A few black 'uh oh' birds kept flying around and occasionally one would swoop in too close for comfort. Danica did not like the 'uh oh' birds any more than she liked the boar hog; they scared the hell out of her even though she knew they were only harmless Fish Crows with their nasally calls that made them sound so weird. However, this day was not quite as terrifying as her first day there, but still, she didn't like it and hoped she would not see that angry looking young native man again. The one that she was sure would kill her.

Danica crossed the river at a fairly safe looking place and hoped to avoid having to swim the deeper areas in the center of the river. No such luck, she ended up swimming across most of it. However, she managed to cross the river without seeing any alligators, only a couple of Great White Egrets that had no interest in her at all. Once on the other side of the river, she walked a short distance down, staying near the bank of the river. At the edge of the river, she saw reachable cattails among the lily pads and decided to get a few for later use. She carefully made her way to them when something on the river caught her attention.

Danica crouched down behind some large cattails that were near a marshy area. She could barely make out the image of a small boat approaching and wasn't sure what to expect, so she decided it was best to stay down and out of sight. Several times she saw movement coming from the boat and then she saw a sharp flash of metal that oddly appeared to be a hat or helmet. Danica thought it looked like the metal hats that Spaniards had worn in the early 1600's when they came here to Florida. She immediately dismissed that thought as being wildly unreasonable because she was just too far away to tell what was happening. A perplexed Danica stayed down and quietly watched this peculiar sight and thought it best to just let the boat pass on by without calling out. Her gut feelings told her that too much was just wrong with this situation.

"Oh, shit!" A low and familiar bellow brought Danica's attention back to her surroundings. All too many times she had heard the mating growls of alligators calling out to a prospective mate, and she knew it was very close.

Danica was shaking uncontrollably and had to figure out something to do or become the alligator's next meal. She didn't want to stand up and attract its attention so she slowly moved behind some tall weeds and palmettos. She felt powerless, and her fear seemed to take over her mind and push her along. These bullying, insistent voices in her head kept telling her to get the hell out of there. But how?

A slight, sharp snapping of twigs told her that the alligator was closer than she had at first thought. She knew there was a chance that the alligator would not attack but just walk on by, and she was not sure she wanted to take that chance. By now, Danica felt certain that the alligator definitely knew she was there. The apprehensive feelings in her gut reaffirmed the alligator's intentions and threatened to shut her down. Sweat mingled with her hair and seemed to intentionally try to blind her left eye. *Ok, stop it, you're obsessing now! And where's my gun when I need it?* Her thoughts raced, *calm down, just calm down.* She didn't dare make any unnecessary movements to brush the hair out of her face.

She waited a few minutes and continued to crouch down, and slowly she moved along the riverbank hoping to put distance between her and the alligator. Just as a precaution, she quickly took her top off to throw over the gator's eyes to blind him - just in case she needed to.

She waited a few more seconds and without warning, he was there, just several feet away. She saw huge, hungry looking eyes, and detected an offensive and disgusting odor that smelled like decaying meat. She was now intensely aware of the alligator's silvery gaze directly fastened on her, and the therapeutic cattails no longer mattered.

He turned his body in the direction of his gaze, and the alligator was on the move. He was demonically advancing towards her exerting all of his strength as he stealthily pushed through the dark slime and cattails towards her. Danica stood upright, but it was too late to run. She heard a rumbling, deep growl, and smelled the oily, putrid 'rot breath' of this hostile enemy that so wanted to take her down.

The giant jaws snapped like a flash of lightening and just missed her arm. Danica's heart was pounding as the monstrous alligator's body thrashed and jerked; his tail tried to batter her and finally knocked her to the ground. Dirt and mud filled her nostrils and mouth. Another low hiss from its throat was even more frightening, and she knew that his next intent was to engage her in the 'death roll', ripping off limbs, and she knew she would never escape that.

72

She felt small and vulnerable as the vicious and hungry creature moved in again to devour his prey.

His eyes glinted angrily while sword-like teeth were ready to chomp down on her to rip her to pieces. Without hesitation, she threw her top over his eyes blinding him just long enough for her to jump up and out of his way. She managed to get behind him and go for his back with outstretched hands. Danica straddled his back and reached around his throat with both arms and her hands forced his mouth down to the ground. Her top no longer covered his eyes, so she carefully slid her right hand up and over his eyes, temporarily blinding him. With her other powerfully strong hand, she held his snout shut and then quickly moved her right hand on down so she was holding his snout shut with both hands. With all of her strength, she pulled his head up and straight back to her chest rendering him powerless until she could get the advantage to a vulnerable spot that was just behind the bump of his head. She saw her chance to go for the vertebrae. What seemed like slow motion must not have been because adrenaline rushed and with tunnel vision, Danica reached for her grandpa's knife and drove it deep into the soft spot of the alligator's neck. She remembered her grandpa's words to *make every thrust powerful and a kill.*

She worked the blade of her knife into the gap of the vertebrae and finished the business without letting up. She used the palm of her hand to drive the knife deep and cut the spinal cord. Danica moved the sharp blade around skillfully and pushed it deep to the bone. She felt the warm blood splatter onto her face. With every ounce of strength she could call forth, she pulled the knife out, and drove it back in again making sure the beast was dead. The pleasurable kill was almost animalistic, as she enjoyed not giving in to her fear.

"It was you or me you slimy bastard, and it ain't me." The jumbled-up words that slurred from her parched lips made her think of something so ridiculous that she laughed out loud for no one to hear.

The alligator's blood was oozing down her cheek now and into her mouth, nauseating her and making her want to gag. This made her think of her tour in Afghanistan and how it didn't prepare her for this. "Give me a break, how hard was being the guard to the nice chaplain? And to go from that uneventful situation to this! This is ridiculous, just ridiculous!" She said out loud again for no one to hear. Her thoughts were undergoing a mistimed explosion that kept banging around inside her head and didn't even make sense. She knew she was bordering on hysterics and had to get a grip on her emotions.

As soon as Danica relaxed her right leg from over the alligator's back leg and tail, she became aware of a shooting pain in her other leg. She loosened the pressure of her left leg that was holding the alligator's left back leg down and moved on away from him. She pulled her pants leg up to see what was going on and saw a large thorn that was embedded at least an inch deep into her thigh. It felt like it was on fire. Danica clinched her teeth and in spite of the pain and watering eyes, she pulled out the offending thorn. She wondered where that had come from and then she remembered seeing a Bougainvillea plant earlier that morning and assumed her clothes had picked it up then.

She carefully looked along the river's edge for burrows with alligator's nests and didn't see any. She calmed down a little and made her way over to the edge of the river to wash off the blood and mud.

She quickly splashed the dark water into her face and onto her leg and was amazed at how good this dark, cloudy water felt to the touch. She made her way back to the cattails to cut a few for her nasty scratches, and out of the corner of her eye, she caught a glimpse of a settler walking towards her. She felt a little nervous at first, but his friendly demeanor put her at ease.

"Hello there. I'm from the settlement down a ways." He took his battered hat off as he approached her.

"Hi." She raised her hand in a little wave.

He continued to approach her, and the manner in which he carried himself was tell-tale of a work weary life in this wilderness. His brown jacket was light, but still seemed a little odd on this warm day. However, all at the same time she knew she needed to keep her arms covered too because of the pesky mosquitoes. His battered hat did seem to become him though, and as he came closer to her, she felt a little more trusting of him.

"I was looking for the settlement. I'm supposed to find a guide there named Elkanah Hawkins. Do you know him?"

"Yes, that's my brother, and I can't believe that you just killed that gator!" She detected a slight British accent.

She nodded.

"And my goodness, you sure do have some lacerations there." He shook his head in disbelief and motioned to his right. "I was working in my cornfield when I heard the commotion. I just thought I'd come see what was going on. Anyway, my name is Jonathan Hawkins and if you want to follow me, my wife can help you out with those scratches and then we'll get Elkanah for you."

"Sure, and my name is Danica. Danica Larsen." She was more than glad to accept his kindness, so she followed him.

CHAPTER 6

The settlement was surprisingly close by and only had about twenty houses. Immediately, Jonathan told several men about the situation with Danica and had them go back to get the alligator. As soon as they brought it into the settlement, some women were waiting and ready to start preparing the meat to smoke. They salted the skin to preserve it for later use, and then they would tan it to sell or trade.

She made a quick assessment about the lifestyle of these people and saw happy children playing nearby in the whitish gray sand under some trees. They didn't seem to have a care in the world, nor did the dog that was relentlessly chasing a squirrel around until it finally ran up a tree to safety.

The wind carried the dull chopping sound of wood through the air, and the tantalizing aroma of cooking bread floated to her nostrils making her mouth water. She could hear voices off in the distance, and the clankity clank of someone shoeing a horse surprised her in this wilderness. They passed a woman that was breaking up a large block of soap, and Danica really wanted a piece of that, but they kept walking. She also heard twigs crunch under her own feet as she walked along trying to keep pace with the tall settler, and she had to admit it, she was beginning to relax some and felt a lot safer in the confines of the small settlement.

Nearby, some other children were in a circle playing 'who has the button', each hoping for a turn to be 'it'. The one appointed 'it' got to stand inside the circle and guess who had the button behind their back. If they had the button, they became 'it'. Then round and round the button went. Their laughter turned into excited whispering at the sight of a stranger entering the settlement. Word was already spreading about how she had killed the alligator and how strange she looked. Danica didn't care if people were looking at her and talking about her; she just wanted to find the lady from the stars and get back home.

Fleur Hawkins was eager to learn more about the new visitor. She was the settler's wife and could barely contain her curiosity as her husband, Jonathan, escorted Danica into their home.

Right away and after introductions, Jonathan had Fleur look at Danica's wounds and help her clean up a bit. She carefully helped her remove the broken white feathers and beads from her tangled hair that was now a mess after the gator incident. Fleur brushed Danica's hair until it was shinier than ever, thanks to the coconut water. Fleur also saw that none of her wounds were serious, but Jonathan was still a little wary of Danica so he took his wife aside and warned her. "She is a strange one, so I wouldn't get so relaxed around her until we know more about her. Why don't you bring her something to eat and then take the kids to the other room and stay there while I talk to her?"

After they went into the other room, he turned to Danica and said, "I saw what you did to that gator back there, but still, I don't think you mean us any harm."

Danica was enjoying a piece of homemade bread with steamy hot soup, so she just shook her head 'no'.

"Just don't use that knife on us, ok? Because you're not in harm's way around here, so go on now, you eat, and then you can tell me about yourself and where you came from?"

Danica paused to speak but Jonathan interrupted. "No, go ahead and eat, then tell me."

Fleur's curiosity brought her back to the kitchen area to serve blackberry cobbler and tea. The children soon followed, one by one. After Fleur had spoon-fed the baby some boiled pears, she turned the spoon over to the baby so she could practice eating on her own. Fleur took off her apron and brushed flour from her long skirt and well-worn white blouse.

Danica saw Fleur approaching the table to sit with her and she noticed traces of flour in her dark hair and wanted to say something, but decided against it. She noticed a small amount on the side of her face and a little in one of her thick black eyebrows. Danica realized that this was the norm for them and decided that it was rather sweet the way she went about cooking for everyone at the large open fireplace that had a large black pot filled with soup. All along the wall beside the fireplace were several pots lined up and ready for use.

After a smiling Fleur had sit down, she leaned in closer to Danica and was eager to talk. Danica saw that her eyes were a warm brown and she could see the genuine kindness in her eyes.

Jonathan knew that Fleur's friendly nature was in charge right now, and she was excited about having a guest. *No need to try and stop her*, he thought and smiled to himself as he went outside to get more wood for the fireplace.

After Jonathan came back inside with a large piece of wood, Fleur filled him in on some of the details about how Danica had the canoeing accident and how she had been in the Army. Even though it was puzzling to Fleur, she still managed to relay the information to him accurately. "Danica said her canoe turned over and she slipped under the blue rainbow that we've all heard about, but she was saying things I didn't quite understand. Things about her being an army guard to a chaplain in some place I've never heard of. Anyway, how can a woman be a guard and in an army?" Her friendly voice had a little bit of a French accent that seemed to tinkle a little like the sound of dainty, high-pitched bells ringing.

She's so charming, and I definitely like her. Danica thought.

"Yes, it is puzzling. However, I did see what she did to that gator." Jonathan was still not quite sure if they should trust her just yet.

"Anyway, I like her and hope she stays for a while. However, she is eager to find her way back home." Fleur called out to the boy and girl, "Ephraim, come help your poppa and bring me some more wood, and Mary, you go help too."

The little one was sweet and they called her Baby Mercy. Danica's heart immediately warmed to see her now joyously rubbing the pears into her hair. Danica felt the genuine kindliness from this family and felt a strong desire to be around them. She had shared with Fleur some facts about her own life. She told her about her mother dying when she was little which made it necessary for her to live with her grandparents. She told her how great it was living with them, but she did miss her mom and never knew her father. She told how he had played the disappearing act before she was even born and didn't know him anyway, but she did feel a definite void there. Her mom had referred to him with contempt as the sperm donor, but she didn't tell Fleur that part or that Danica considered him another disappointment, just like Alex.

In return, Fleur sadly shared the fate of her family and a few others that had no idea of what was in store for them in this new country. They had been the only survivors of a French Huguenot colony that had been massacred by the Spaniards. "Luckily for my family and the others, they were taken in by some nearby natives in the area that showed compassion. Later, they ended up here. That was before I was born. I was born here in this settlement, and the natives are friendly towards us here, so we stay," Fleur said.

"Oh, do you have more family here now?"

"Not anymore." Fleur looked sad again. "It sometimes gets lonely."

"I know and that must have been horrible for your family to experience the massacre."

"Yes, they said it was horrible. The Captain-General of the Spaniards ordered our ships to be destroyed, but they didn't have to because there was a high wind that destroyed them anyway. They burned our colony and believed that all were dead, and the one's they didn't kill, they took as prisoners to never be heard from again.

"My family, actually, it was my grandparents and a few others saw a flag hoisted on one of the Spanish ships and knew it was a war signal, so they hid as far into the woods as they could go and waded in knee-deep water to stay alive. They wandered for days and had no bread or provisions. They were finally able to find a secure place to fish and feed themselves for a day or so and then they kept moving inward and finally some friendly natives noticed them and took them in.

"It was a harrowing experience that reached to their very souls. They always hoped that someone would come looking for them, but they never did."

Danica could hear the sadness in Fleur's voice but she wanted to hear more so she asked. "That's sad, but why did the Spaniards want to destroy your colony?"

"Because they wanted to claim this land for Spain and they hated everyone in the colony for being Protestants. They called them the Lutherans. "

"I'm sorry your family went through that. So then, are most of the people in this village French?"

"Oh no, we take in others as they come along." Fleur said.

Danica was beginning to feel comfortable with Fleur, so she mentioned the woman with the soap. The one she had passed coming into the settlement. She asked, "Do you think she would give me a piece of it?"

"Yes, except I have something milder. She makes that soap for the whole settlement, for our clothes. I make the milder soap for our skin, for bathing." She handed Danica a piece. "Here, this smells better too."

"Wow, how did you make it smell so good?" Danica smiled and tucked it into a pocket.

Fleur smiled. "Fragrant oils that Jonathan's father would get for me. Jonathan's father was the Indian Trader to these parts and he would bring us all sorts of things when the ships would come in."

"That's interesting, but what would he trade?" Danica asked.

"Many different things. He would trade useful items such as tools, shovels, fabrics, and fragrant oils to the Indians for their furs."

"Really?"

"Oh yes. He would also trade coffee, axes, and almost anything. And then, he would supply the furs to Europeans to make their hats and coats. They love fur collars and cuffs. That's how I got these pretty cups, from his father."

Danica quickly forgot the soap when the door slowly opened, and she saw the fur headpiece first. It was the headpiece with the red and white cloth that was securely wrapped around the loose topknot. And then, the yellowish tan feathers with white tinges became visible. She felt petrified to the spot.

The person coming through the door had to lower his head to come through, and then his big frame filled the entrance. She recoiled in fear when the strange person with angry eyes came inside the house. She recognized him as the same person that had pulled her out of the river that unforgettable day when her canoe had turned over. Danica felt fear take over when she smelled that same strange oily smell of a hunter or something else indistinguishable, and her hand instinctively went for her knife.

"Hold on Danica, this is my brother. He's not going to hurt you," Jonathan said, waving his hand. "Put that away."

"He doesn't look like your brother," she said and never took her eyes off this large man that was slowly approaching her. She was trembling from fear, and her heart raced but she did as Jonathan said and put her knife back into its sheath. This fearsome man's dark eyes followed her every move again as he continued to move in closer and came alarmingly near until he was towering over her.

Jonathan saw her distress and said, "This is Elkanah Hawkins that you were looking for, and he is indeed my brother."

She said again, "He doesn't look like your brother."

"Yes, I know we don't look like brothers, but we are. We had different mothers, but the same father and the same last name. He'll be the guide to take you to the woman you are looking for."

"Oh, hell no he won't!" The words just flew out of Danica's mouth before she could refrain from commenting.

Jonathan saw the fear in her eyes so he proceeded to say, "Elkanah's mother is Timucuan Indian from a village up north from here; some say she's described as being a woman of an indomitable spirit, but even so, she will help you. You'll pass through her village on the way to find this woman you are looking for."

Jonathan could still see that she was not convinced. "Our father was British and the Indian Trader to these parts. He came here from Virginia. Elkanah is of mixed blood and that's why he is accepted among most tribes. My mother was one of the settlers here and life was hard for her. She died from a fever at an early age and then our father married Elkanah's mother; her name is Sushaney."

She flinched when she saw this big man move in even closer to her, and she could tell that her appearance was clearly puzzling to him. His eyes never came off her, and he took in every inch of her. She saw his eyes move slowly over her and down to her feet. She saw him take another glance at the cargo pants she was wearing as if the pockets puzzled him. Her black printed tee shirt seemed to be just as interesting to him as he looked closer at the fading ink print of two small kittens. Earlier she had taken off the outer shirt the old woman had given to her because of the warmth from the fireplace.

"You do make me inquisitive." Elkanah made a slight gesture with his hand when he questioned her. "How does such a little one kill the fierce gator like you did?" Word of the kill had spread, and now his dark eyes seemed to look right through her hazel eyes as if he was trying to figure out what kind of woman she was, and this terrified her.

"I've seen it done."

Each movement he made caused a rustling sound to come from his headdress, and the sound of clothing brushing against leather mesmerized her. It was as if he had just stepped out of a history book and was moving towards her. She was so enthralled and terrified at the same time by his appearance that she began to feel panic rising in her chest again.

Fleur walked over to Danica. She placed her arm around her and said in a reassuring way, "I promise you that you will be safe in Elkanah's care. He will protect you."

"He doesn't look safe."

Fleur gently said, "He is safe, so try to relax and tomorrow morning after breakfast you can get an early start. You'll be fine. If anybody can get you to the lady you are looking for, it is Elkanah."

"Okay."

Fleur gave her another hug and then turned to Elkanah. "She'll be okay. She just seems a little nervous after what she's been through. You must be hungry. Come over here and sit down and I'll bring you something."

Relief washed over Danica when Fleur got Elkanah's attention away from her. She didn't think she could take any more of his dark looks that evening and was glad when he walked away from her.

Fleur brought Elkanah and Jonathan a bowl of hot winter squash soup and bread, and then she offered more cobbler and hot tea to Danica, which she gladly accepted. She made it a point to sit far to the other end of the table, away from the large man. Nothing else was mentioned again about the lady from the stars and Elkanah left shortly after the meal, without even looking her way again.

Fleur made Danica as comfortable as possible, and she did genuinely seem to be worried about her well-being.

CHAPTER 7

It was raining again the next morning as they discussed the dilemma that Danica was in, and how she might find the lady and get back to her home. Jonathan and Elkanah also discussed with her the dangers of going through the forest and the confrontations with hostile Indians that was sure to come.

"I can take you to the Spanish mission to see the Franciscan Friar there. He says he has personally seen the lady from the stars that you are looking for, and he will tell us how to get to her," Elkanah said.

Jonathan still saw some fear in Danica's eyes so he sympathetically offered more reassurance. "No need to fear Elkanah. He's safe and will take you there. You can't go alone because you would never survive."

Danica reluctantly agreed and in spite of the wet and soggy conditions outside, they departed as soon as the rain stopped. She still didn't quite trust him though and couldn't seem to get beyond her fear of him.

After they left Jonathan's house, and as they were walking towards the outer areas of the settlement, Danica finally got up the nerve to talk to him. "Where is this mission, and how long will it take to get there?"

Elkanah continued walking and never looked at her. His serious demeanor never changed. "About five days and you can relax, I'm not going to do anything to you."

"Okay." She hoped she could trust him. Her gut seemed to be up in her throat at the thoughts of going into the forest alone with this man. She nervously thought, a*nd God only knows for sure how many days and nights I'll be alone with him. He'll probably kill me in my sleep.* She shuddered to think about it and almost decided to stay at the settlement with Fleur and Jonathan, but she knew she would never get home if she didn't take this chance and go with him.

"My mother's village is even farther away from here and we will be able to rest there until the other two guides come back through there. When they arrive, we will have them join us. Their names are William and Moses, and like me, their mothers are also Timucuan and their fathers were Indian Traders from Virginia, just like my father. I'm telling you this just so you'll know what to expect."

"Okay, but I'm not sure I know what you mean about them being Indian Traders. Fleur mentioned it, but I didn't really understand. What do they do?"

"The Europeans want furs and the Indian Traders meet at certain trading points to barter with native trappers for their furs. We just try to avoid the pirates, so we stay back and out of their way and try to not let them see us.

"Pirates?"

He nodded.

All of this talk about fur traders and pirates puzzled her because she still didn't understand about the Blue Rainbow and how she got here. In fact, she didn't know where she was. It was just as peculiar to the inhabitants of this place as it was to her because they didn't even know her time and place existed. They were all just as mystified by all of this as she was.

Elkanah had to duck to go under some low hanging vines that covered most of the trees at the edge of the settlement. The leaves were still wet from the last rain that morning and Elkanah showed no signs of letting that stop him, so Danica quietly followed and listened with intense curiosity while he explained more about William and Moses.

"Interesting, but I'm just curious about something," she said.

"What's that?" He still didn't look at her but continued walking.

"You and Jonathan are brothers but you look nothing alike. I know he explained about your mothers, but I'm still trying to figure it out. You know, Jonathan's a settler and you're an Indian guide. Why such a difference?"

"We told you. It's because I was raised in my mother's village, and he was raised in this settlement. They say I look a lot like my

90

mother, and he is light skinned like our father was. I took my mother's Timucuan ways, which is our custom. However, I had a lot of my father's influence growing up, and Jonathan and I both spent time with him when he would barter for furs. He would usually barter for huge amounts of furs at one time and then they would be loaded onto large ships. Jonathan, as well as Fleur, are somewhat older than I am, but even so, we are very close and much alike in many ways. We both loved our father a great deal and Chua killed him. And I've just received word that Chua has also killed my grandfather from my mother's village, and I am on my way to kill him."

She gasped in horror at his direct truthfulness.

"Also, if you want to reach this lady you are looking for, we have to be rid of Chua and his warriors first to get through to where she is."

She nodded and felt a chill go over her. She was beginning to understand the dark looks that she had been seeing in Elkanah's eyes. He was pissed, and wanted Chua's blood to flow.

"Then why are you even bothering to take me along? Won't I be in the way?"

"Because Fleur wants me to help you and besides that, after the way you killed that gator, I have decided that you will be useful to have around." He still didn't look at her. "Knowing this, do you still want to go?"

"Yes."

"Well, okay. And, watch out, don't let that spider get on you." He reached out and brushed it off a low hanging limb with the backside of his hand.

It was a nasty looking thing, and larger than any she had ever seen. "Thanks."

They walked in silence for a few minutes and Elkanah finally looked at her. "We will go through some rough terrain with much dense stands of trees and wild animals. It won't be a very smooth journey and it will be tiresome. Do you think you can make it? If not, you can stay at the settlement with Jonathan and Fleur."

"I'll go." Danica answered knowing this was her only chance to return home.

Elkanah nodded. "Good, I thought so."

She thought she saw a spark of amusement in his eyes, and just as quickly, the troubled look was back.

After they were a short distance from the settlement, Elkanah was also curious about her. "I did try to find you that first day you were here. Where did you go when you ran off?"

"I hid in the trees." She paused. "Literally, in the trees."

"But how did you survive?"

"The first three days I ate bananas and figs, and then I found a beach close by that had lots of clams and luckily for me I knew how to start a fire."

"Okay," he said.

"After that I found crabs and other types of seafood. And get this, the people in the nearby village were friendly to me and an old lady gave me these moccasins and top."

He suddenly stopped and said in surprise. "Really?" He leaned in so close to her that she could have touched his multi-colored shirt if she had wanted to, but she didn't want to be that close to him. She felt like the life was going out of her as he came in even closer and took another step towards her. All she was aware of was the way his presence and his energy seemed to sweep over her and cover her completely. Then she could actually smell a musky odor each time he moved, and the smell of leather was not to her disliking. His feathers in his headpiece were shining in the morning sun and the raccoon tail shifted slightly each time he moved his head. Just over his right eye were several small scars that she had not noticed before and one larger one going into his hairline. He was ruggedly attractive with a strong, clear bone structure. She stood frozen in this terrifying moment and had conflicting feelings about going forward with this strange man, but resisted the urge to run away from him again.

"You're lucky is all I have to say."

"Why?"

"Because these friendly people you mention are not always so
   friendly," he said.

"It's good for you that you like to dance. They killed the others
   that wouldn't dance."

"You're joking!" Danica said.

"No, I'm not joking. They just liked it because you danced with
them. It would have been an insult to not dance with them and they
would have killed you too." He appeared even more threatening the
closer he came in to her. He was looking down at her with looks that
said he was even more amused and mystified by her now than ever
before.

"So, where did you find shelter from the rain?" He was still
curious to know.

"Really, like I said, in the trees and a nearby cave. I'll show you
when we pass through that way." They had to backtrack a little to get
onto a more traveled trail. "Anyway, I want to see Rose Marie again.
She's a monkey and very sweet," she said.

He nodded. "Well anyway, it might get a little colder as we go
north of here, so I thought this would help you to stay warm if you
need it." His hand reached inside the large well-worn leather pouch
that he had casually draped over his shoulder. It had three hellacious
animal teeth dangling on leather strips from the flap.

She watched in amazed disbelief as he pulled a rolled up and
beautiful Lynx fur from the pouch. It was soft to the touch and felt
luxurious even in this wilderness. She accepted it with gratitude.

94

She nodded and lowly said. "Thanks." She threw it over her shoulder realizing that he had purposefully brought it for her comfort and this left her with mixed emotions like never before. How could someone so fierce do something so thoughtful? The conflicting emotions were tearing at her thoughts. She wanted to trust him, but she was afraid to.

The soft Lynx fur felt good against her skin and she realized that the scents of hides and leather were much to her liking. She was beginning to feel oddly comforted and safe by these strong odors that she was realizing to be distinctive of Elkanah.

He started walking again through an overgrown path that was only wide enough for one person at a time. He brushed through the large palmettos that were hanging every which way and even over the path where they traveled. She walked behind him and couldn't help but admire the craftsmanship of the sheath that dangled across his back. It hung in a way that would make it easy to tilt forward if he needed to draw his spear quickly.

When they reached the trees, they didn't hang around there too long. They were eager to move along on their journey to find the lady from the stars. Elkanah followed Danica as she stepped onto a large limb that almost touched the ground in places. Other low hanging limbs made it easy to climb higher and higher until they reached her shelter.

"Make yourself at home." Danica motioned towards her shelter, and from the approving look on Elkanah's face she could tell that he was feeling the same freeness she felt and it was not bad. Right away, she noticed him examining her over-sized hammock, and with an extremely puzzled look on his face.

"Get in it. Try it out." Danica said with a little hint of a smile.

Before he could answer she said, "Here like this," and she steadied it by holding it with one hand and carefully moved over into it and reclined. She got back out of it and said, "Here, you try it."

She steadied it while he moved over into the hammock and reclined. She gave it a little shove and it gently moved back and forth.

"Not bad, but we have to go." He gently reached and grabbed a sturdy limb to stop the movement of the hammock and to steady himself so he was able to step out of it and onto the larger limb.

About that time Rose Marie made her appearance and affectionately moved in closer to Danica. She stroked the monkey a few times and said, "Look what I found for you." Danica pulled a pear out of her pocket and sliced off a piece for her. This special treat excited Rose Marie so much that she pushed in closer for another piece.

They rested for a few more minutes, and Danica showed Elkanah the shells she had gathered while down at the beach. After thirty minutes or so, they took off for the mission, waving goodbye to Rose Marie.

They hiked through some damp areas and the wet, cool ground had the scent of rotting tree trunks that had fallen to the ground, and on up the path the sweet and refreshing smells of pine needles floated through the air. That reminded Danica of her grandpa and Josh. She felt sad and missed them. She had hoped she would be with them by Christmas time, but that seemed doubtful now. She was beginning to hear the faint musical sounds that some birds were making and it was soothing to her ears. As they walked along it was clear to her that they were approaching a small flock of birds, but when they came too near, they all flew away. She watched in silence until they were totally out of sight and wondered why she had never noticed the beauty of birds in flight before. "Awesome," she said out loud.

"What's awesome?" Elkanah glanced at her with a puzzled look.

"The birds."

He nodded and kept walking.

She was getting tired and her feet hurt, but complaining was not an option. Elkanah didn't show any signs of fatigue, so she kept walking. They came to an area where a thick cushion of pine needles and pinecones covered the path and she was glad when they got past that. It was just aggravating trying to step over and around the pinecones and pine needles because of the prickles.

She couldn't tell how many hours they had been walking when they smelled animal dung, and it was fresh in the air. One thing was for sure because of her time spent in the trees, she had learned that deer and bear have different smells. She looked around, saw a pile of deer pellets, and knew that a deer was definitely in close proximity to them. Before she had a chance to say anything, Elkanah drew his powerful spear–it happened so fast–he balanced it, brought it back to his ear, and then threw it. The slicing sound the point of his spear made filled the air. The deer fell in its tracks, and immediately Danica started gathering twigs to make a fire while Elkanah skinned the deer. It was truly tasty and the first that Danica had ever eaten.

Later, they passed a strange looking sight. It was an old lady with stringy hair and real dirty clothes. She was just sitting there beside a creek and as soon as she saw them, she ran away.

"What the heck?" Danica was surprised to say the least.

"It's Anna. She's harmless, just strange."

"But who is she?"

"Don't know. She just lives in the woods."

"How sad. How long has she been living in the woods?"

"I don't know. As long as I can remember."

They kept walking, and Elkanah didn't say anything else about Anna, so Danica didn't either.

CHAPTER 8

They silently walked for about four hours and then came upon a gruesome sight. Everywhere, everywhere were bodies. They saw bodies of men, women, and children that were heavy with bloat and dust. Indians as well as a few settlers that had red scarves tied around their necks that indicated they were friendly to the Indians.

Many were in fields that had been crushed down from the weight of bodies on top of bodies. It was as if they had been huddled there together, and hiding. Flies were laying their eggs in nostrils, eyes, ears, open wounds and any other opening they could find. The stink of blood soaked, urine-stained clothes touched Danica's senses and made her want to drop and die here too.

In the distance, she saw others and panicked at the sight of more dead bodies that had been wasted from starvation and dehydration. Death and decay were thick in the air. The putrefying smells caused Danica to vomit until her ribs ached. Stooping or more like crumpling to the ground, Danica tried to keep her mind from going there and visualizing what had happened to those poor wretched souls. The sight of decomposing flesh was almost more than she could bear, and these unlucky corpses could certainly never tell what had overcome them.

Out of the corner of her eye, she saw a body that was lying halfway across another body, and a flicker of movement made her realize that there was still life left in this 'pathetic remains' of a man. Dry dirt was sticking to his face and in words barely audible, he lowly said, "They were just wolves to us, filthy wolves." The settler's gaze was fixated on a fly that just wouldn't go away and then he dropped off into a forever sleep. She forced herself to get up and inch in closer to him. It was gut wrenching to be so close to death and even as horrific as this was, she reluctantly picked up a skinning knife that had dropped from his weathered hand. This weathered hand that was so indicative of a hard life in this wilderness did not need the knife any longer, but she accepted the fact that she did. Close by, she noticed some leather strips and wrapped them several times around her left leg making a temporary knife sheath inside her moccasin.

The stillness was haunting, and it was hot. She wanted the sun to stop blazing. A rooster was aimlessly walking around, *and who cares about a rooster,* she thought. She couldn't stop crying, and slowly walked past pots of honey and a piece of wood with a saw still wedged into the middle of it. Up ahead, more wood and honey had dropped to the ground for no one to care about or ever use again.

Even though she was dazed, she continued to push forward and found more ruination and destruction. Eventually she came to a place at the far side of the settlement where something silly looking kept moving around in a weird and ungainly way beside some tall bushes. Upon closer inspection, she realized that it was only part of an unlucky settler's clumsily built clothesline with a shirt flapping in the breeze. She fought hysteria as hot tears slid down her face.

When she was just past the makeshift clothesline, a wild man jumped out from nowhere. Half of his jaw was hanging off and blood oozed from the right side of his head. His ripped and frayed uniform vaguely resembled the ones worn by the Spanish Conquistadors that Danica recalled seeing in history books when she was a child.

Her head was spinning as the sound of a pathetic dog howling off in the distance sickened her even more. She had the fleeting thought that he would either die here too, or join a pack of wild dogs to survive this land.

The dying man screamed in agony and was clearly out of his mind. He fell towards her desperately trying to claw at her face and hair. His bloody hands on her made her weak with fear and she knew she had no choice but to kill him. Her hand felt oddly at ease as she reached for her grandpa's knife on her hip and mercifully put him to rest. Now void of emotions, she dropped to her knees and pulled her knife from his throat just above his breastplate. A calmness came over her revealing to her that she would kill again to survive. As she realized this truth, all traces of fear left her.

Her mind went back to the day she had killed the alligator and realized that indeed, the odd sight she had seen on the river that day was probably a Conquistador. She was more puzzled now than ever.

Her legs began to tremble with weakness as she managed to raise herself to a standing position. Her shaky legs tried to go forward, but she was too weak to move. She fell back to the ground and as she was falling, she saw a Spaniard's helmet resting in a patch of weeds confirming to her that he was indeed a Spanish conquistador. She managed to get to her feet again and noticed that he had two leather arm bracers. Just why he had two bracers she didn't know, but she removed them and put them on her own arms. It just seemed common logic to her now that she needed them now more than he did. His crossbow and arrows were just a few yards away in a thicket of small trees and bushes.

A dazed Danica was now armed, tired, and thirsty as she set out to look for Elkanah. She saw him approaching her from the edge of a field of corn. They were separated for a short time as they assessed the damage that had been inflicted upon this settlement. Elkanah had seen her remove the arm bracers from the Spaniard's wrists and put them on her own as he was approaching her. He then saw her pick up the bow and arrows.

When he got closer to her, he saw the blood on her hands and then ran quickly to her. "Are you okay?" he said as he looked down at the Spaniard.

She nodded and with no emotion at all she said, "I killed him."

He said with concern in his voice, "What happened?"

"He jumped out at me and tried to rip my face off so I killed him. He was crazy and his jaw was hanging off." She felt tired and brushed loose, tangled hair out of her face. Some strands of her hair were beginning to dry in the residue of the Spaniard's blood that his bloody hands had smeared on her face.

"I see." Elkanah frowned a little as he contemplated her answer. "You do make me wonder about the place you came from. Jonathan said you were a guard in an army. What kind of place is this that a woman can be in an army? I don't really understand."

"Right, I was in the army. Where I come from a woman can enlist in the military to help protect our country. I was in a place called Afghanistan, but I didn't see any action," she said.

"You mean a woman warrior?" he said in disbelief. "You mean military is like our warriors that protect our villages and go to war?"

"Yes, I guess you could say that."

"The other women in the settlement, Fleur and the others are somewhat different from you, but I guess this is okay." Elkanah was trying to understand her ways. "Some of our Timucuan women have engaged in battle when our villages were being attacked."

Danica could tell that he was trying to mentally process this unusual concept.

"Did you see a spring or lake nearby? I need some water." She wiped sweat and dirt out of her face. "I feel like I'm getting dehydrated."

"Yes, come with me and I'll take you to it." Elkanah turned and led the way back to a nearby spring where they rested for a while. It was a blessed relief to Danica when she saw the clear water that was very welcomed and cool to her parched lips and dry throat. She filled her water bottle several times and thought she would never get enough of it.

"I assume you can use the weapon you equipped yourself with." He looked at her with a questioning look and slightly raised brows.

She nodded, "I've used a smaller one, but I'll get used to this one."

"Well, before we leave here, I'm going to make sure you can use it. We're going through a dense forest and there will be a lot of wild animals and you'll need to know how to use it." Elkanah picked up a shell club that a dead warrior no longer needed. "Here, do you know how to throw this?"

"No."

"Okay, I'll show you."

She slipped it down into the waistband of the right side of her pants.

The bow and quiver of arrows were quite large, but immediately she felt comfortable with it. The club had a wooden handle with a conch shell for the blade and could slice through an animal or a person with one powerful thrust. Danica practiced with her right hand and then her left hand throwing it and knew instantly that this would be her best friend. She carefully lowered it to her knee, then back up over her shoulder and then the 'thrust'. She did this over and over with both hands until she was at ease with it. She also learned the proper way of throwing it with both hands by pulling it back behind her head and then with as much force as possible she plunged the club into a tree. Elkanah nodded his approval.

After Elkanah was sure that Danica was proficient at using the weaponry, they went again to the back of the settlement where the spring was located. They both took advantage of the crystal-clear water to rid themselves of some grime and blood. Danica took her moccasins off and waded into the water with her clothes on for a quick bath. Fleur's soap was heavenly. She washed her colorful top with the soap and hung it over a branch to dry in the hot sun.

The soap made her skin feel silky smooth and it made her hair soft too, but she sucked in her breath in surprise when she saw Elkanah unashamedly bathing nude in her presence. His muscular shoulders glistened in the afternoon sun and his long, wet hair was sleek and smooth flowing down his tattooed back. Her eyes followed the tattoos all the way down his backside to his tattooed thighs, which ended at the water line of the spring. She let her breath out and quickly looked the other way in confusion and embarrassment before he could see her looking. She realized that this was the normal thing to do among these beautiful people so she removed her cargo pants and T-shirt to dry them on a branch. She decided to let her sports bra and panties dry on her body. Elkanah didn't seem to notice either way.

Her clothes were almost dry when she put them back on because they didn't want to waste any more time there just lingering. Elkanah had said the forest was dense, and they should leave to get through it before dark. He was right; the forest was dense and trekking through the heavy woods almost got the best of her. She felt pain as branches reached out and slapped her in the face leaving a nasty scratch, but they pushed through them anyway as they trampled small bushes under their feet. However, Danica welcomed the sweet and refreshing conifer smells of the forest that purged her memory of the obnoxious odors of death that had threatened to linger in her thoughts and nasal passages.

About two hours out of the settlement, they met a man with a funny looking hat. It was perched right on the top of his head and Danica wondered how it stayed on because it was clearly too small for his head.

"Good day." He greeted them.

"Where are you headed?" Elkanah asked.

"Back to the settlement. I've been at the mission. I had to see if I could find some medicine for my wife. She's been sick for too long with a fever of some sort."

Danica and Elkanah both realized that the poor man would not find his wife alive. Danica dropped her head and looked away.

Elkanah spoke, "We just came through there, and I'm afraid it didn't go well for them. They were attacked, and I'm sorry to say they are all dead. Maybe you should come with us and go back to the mission."

A look of horror washed over the man's face and he ran off towards the settlement.

Danica and Elkanah sadly moved forward with a heavy heart for the man, but they knew there was absolutely nothing they could do for him.

It seemed like they walked for hours and she finally asked, "How much farther to the mission?"

"Not too far, we'll make a fire soon and rest."

The next morning, they didn't linger there too long because they both wanted to get to the mission. After going a short distance down the trail, something suddenly startled Danica as it dove out at her. It clutched at the side of her shoulder and just hung on and wouldn't let go. She screeched as she jumped around trying to shake it off. Just that quickly, Elkanah grabbed the thing between his fingers, pinched it around the back of its neck, and removed it from her shoulder. It was a creepy looking lizard.

"Get out of here." Elkanah threw the disgusting looking thing into the woods on the other side of the path. He didn't even look at her, he just started walking again as if nothing had happened.

She trudged along behind Elkanah without saying a word about the harsh and burdensome conditions of the forest. The path was so narrow that they had to go single file and it seemed that they were going deeper than ever into the forest.

Elkanah suddenly stopped and motioned for her to be silent. Something just felt unnatural about the moment that threatened to go on forever without end. She stood motionless waiting for a signal from Elkanah.

Out of nowhere came three native men and blocked the path in front of them. They had extreme headdresses with brightly colored feathers and fabrics. Their clothes were of more brightly colored fabrics and quite beautiful. These splendid men waited in a patient manner as Elkanah and Danica approached them. Elkanah spoke first, and in a language unknown to her. All seemed friendly enough and they passed through the area without problems.

"What was that all about?"

"We're passing through parts of their village and they were greeting us as we passed through."

"Nice."

CHAPTER 9

When they finally reached the mission, it was late in the evening on the fifth day of their journey and they were still damp from another downpour. "Will it ever quit raining?" she asked.

Elkanah shrugged. "Eventually, sometimes it just rains a lot."

As they were approaching the mission, she saw that it was gloomy and enclosed by a high wall with two large stone pillars on both sides of the gate. She couldn't help but wonder if it was a good idea for them to be there because as they came up to the mission there was obvious tension among the friars and Indians. The native people were openly laughing and making fun of a friar that had come outside of the mission to talk to them about salvation and the eternity of their souls. He was encouraging them to come to the services on Sunday. They were not willing to do that or accept the friar's beliefs about religion and had responded by turning around and exposing their naked butts to the friar. Danica smirked a little and just looked down and shook her head as they walked on past the situation.

Once they were past the commotion, she glanced over at Elkanah to see what his reaction was and he hadn't seemed to notice what had just taken place. Danica couldn't help but grin now and thought, *well, alrighty then, how would he know about mooning?* She managed to 'not laugh' out loud at this thought.

They kept walking towards the mission gate and tried to avoid attracting attention to themselves because of the intensity of agitation that was going on at the moment. It seemed peculiar to Danica to see a few small houses scattered out among the trees just outside the mission.

"Who lives in these houses? she had to ask but in almost a whisper.

"Some natives that have turned to Christianity. They live here to better learn the Christian ways and to learn to read and write. It's a very clear advantage to be able to read and write."

"Yes, for sure," she said.

"See those kids over there?" Elkanah motioned towards five native children walking with a friar towards the entrance gate to the mission.

Danica nodded.

"They will be here for a while to learn to read and write. I was here also as a child, but my father taught me many things also."

When they finally reached the entrance gate, they passed through the two large pillars that were on each side of the gate, and once inside, Danica noticed over to her right, a small cemetery with several wooden markers. One had fresh dirt and a new marker made out of wood and in the shape of a cross. A friar was lingering there having a private moment of thoughtfulness. In his hands was a large wooden cross that had been roughly carved into a necklace with an enlarged hole for a piece of twine. The twine was looped through his fingers as if he had been praying for quite some time.

After they made their way past the cemetery, they came to a stone building that had several pear trees beside it and about that time, another friar came out and welcomed them. His simple brown robe was a wee bit too long and touched the ground in the back. The robe had a very plain and frayed cincture that hung almost down to his feet. Danica thought it odd that he was such a slight built man. *Barely larger than a twelve-year old boy*, she thought, but it was obvious by his friendly nature that Elkanah had met him on many other occasions. He led them past a huge bell tower and then past the friary. The bell was silent at the moment, but Danica was curious to know about the sounds that were sure to come from it soon.

They walked on past the counsel house, and into the chapel that had ornate carvings throughout it, but no benches. That seemed out of the ordinary to Danica, but she didn't question it. He then led them past a table that had different religious items such as crucifixes, holy water, and coral prayer beads. He didn't stop there though, and seemed completely oblivious to everything around him as he led them on out and through a long hallway to a large living area.

It would have been gloomy in the chapel and the living area if it had not been for the large candles that they kept lit even during the day. They had long ropes extending down from the ceiling with large pieces of wood tied together making a shelf above the table. This shelf held several larger candles and provided adequate lighting, much to Danica's amazement.

The smell of freshly chopped wood was lingering in the air and it made her think of the chickens they had just passed before entering the chapel. The poor little things just walked around the yards freely and without purpose or direction not knowing that they would be a meal soon.

She told her story over again to the friar and he looked pained to hear it. He was exceptionally kind to Danica and sympathetic to her situation. The friar told them to go north from the village where Elkanah's mother lives, and into a large uninhabited wilderness that separates two huge chiefdoms; from the second village they were to go west for a short distance by raft down a river that would empty into the gulf. There they would find another mission and the friar would give them shelter and tell them exactly how to get to the lady from the stars.

The good friar had carefully mapped out the way to the other mission for Elkanah because it was a new mission and he had never been there before. It seemed a little odd to Danica that the Spanish friars would be so friendly to them when it was also so obvious that there was conflict between the natives and some Spanish Conquistadors. It just didn't make sense to Danica.

Later Danica cleaned herself up the best she could and by now, her clothes had dried out. She was startled at her own reflection in the friar's mirror. Her light brown hair was slightly tangled and her wooden comb didn't help a whole lot. *Some nice shampoo and conditioner would be a good thing;* she thought of the coconut water and wished she had some right now for conditioner.

After she combed her hair the best she could, she pulled it back and made one braid, then securely tied it with some leather she had picked up at the massacre site. She couldn't resist the urge to twist a dreadlock and let it dangle down the right side of her head. She thought it looked okay but she mainly wanted her hair out of her face because it was getting rather long. Thanks to the Aloe, she saw that her skin was still looking smooth, but she thought that a little makeup would be a good thing.

The friar made them comfortable for the evening and brought out rabbit stew with mushrooms, carrots, and potatoes. The stew had a different taste and was nothing like the beef stew that her grandma used to make, but it was still very good. To Danica's surprise, the friar used many different herbs and spices and when he brought out a tray with three large glasses of wine to go with the never-ending tray of bread with olive oil for dipping, her jaw dropped. The thought of the Godly friar consuming anything alcoholic was surprising to her.

Elkanah saw Danica's questioning looks when she saw the friar bring out the wine. He leaned in closer to Danica and explained, "the water here has a bad taste, so drink the wine."

She saw that Elkanah and the friar were already enjoying their wine, so she assured him, "Not a problem. Just what I wanted."

He learned over closer to her again and almost in a whisper, "The friar says it's okay for a person to drink the wine here, but not to become drunken because it's a sin to do that."

"Okay, I won't." She suppressed a giggle and thought the wine might be 'butt kicking', just like grandpa's homemade wine, but it had a sweet taste a lot like grape juice.

She quietly sipped her wine and watched Elkanah converse with the good friar. The conversation was mostly about the other mission and the friar there. She continued to sip her wine and study Elkanah's habitual gestures and his way of speaking. His impeccable English and mannerisms fascinated her; he was not at all like her first impression of him the day she thought he would surely kill her. At least, she hoped not.

Later, the kind friar showed them each to a separate and very small room with a bed that actually had a bed frame and a thin mattress - a very thin mattress. Again, she thought of the poor little chickens that would probably become a feather mattress soon. *Poor little things*, she thought and almost giggled again suspecting that the friar's wine was a little high proof too, just like Grandpa's.

She relaxed and was appreciative of the bed and the friar's kindness, but then she heard some crickets begin to chirp. Their chirping was getting a little louder and getting on her nerves. She wondered where it was coming from and then she remembered that there was a small window just outside the door of her room. After a while, she thought, *shut up already, and get a mate*! Eventually they were silent and she was relieved that they had probably found the perfect mate and now she could rest.

The next morning a different friar assisted them by serving them breakfast and strangely, there was a jar of olives on the table to go with it. This did seem odd to have olives for breakfast, but it wasn't bad.

Afterwards, Danica and Elkanah set out to look for the friar they had been with the day before. They wanted to thank him for the kind way he had treated them and for telling them how to find the other mission. However, before they found him, many interesting copper plate engravings that were staggered all along the walls distracted Danica. She found them to be so interesting that she couldn't resist the urge to examine each one. The large one, and it appeared to be the most important one, had an engraving of a man and below his image it said, 'Blessed is the man who TRUSTS in the Lord'. Another copper plate had several images of men that she assumed were important church figures. Also, along the walls were framed maps of places unknown to her; these hung on long chains that extended from beams coming out from the ceiling. Each beam had ropes carefully wrapped around them to keep them in place. It was unusual but interesting all at the same time. She had the feeling that she was in a museum and the artisanship of each piece was stunning.

"Ready?" Elkanah managed to get her attention.

"Sure." But she was reluctant to leave the beauty of this area of the mission.

"By the way, does the friar have a name?" Elkanah had just referred to him as the friar.

"Yes, it is James."

"Oh."

They finally found Friar James in a small room just off the chapel. They chatted with him for a while and she noticed his Gregorian calendar on the wall behind him. It said September 17, 1624. Danica had an uneasy feeling in the pit of her stomach and felt like she couldn't breathe. She knew, right then and there that she was screwed.

CHAPTER 10

After they left the mission, they headed northeast towards the village where Elkanah's mother lived. They passed through some grassy areas at first, and then there was a steady rain, but Elkanah kept moving forward and obviously had no intentions of stopping because of it.

They bogged down in mud almost to their knees in one area, but they still kept moving. It was tiresome to Danica as the rain relentlessly refused to let up, but they managed to make their way through some very dense areas. They had to chop away some high growth so they could pass through unpredictable areas that were sure to have some extremely dangerous animals. Finally, relief came and the rain stopped.

Danica saw it first. A huge Lynx was poised and ready to lunge at the uninvited strangers. Danica carefully raised her bow and arrow towards the thick limb that the Lynx was resting on. With a sudden thrust of its body, the Lynx was flying through the air towards them and just as quickly her arrow sliced through its body. It dropped with a dull, heavy thud just inches from them. Just to make sure it was no more of a threat, Danica put another arrow into the side of its head.

"Hurry, let's skin it and get out of here," Elkanah said. They didn't waste any time leaving in case another Lynx should come along. Elkanah knew that a Lynx will usually travel alone, but it's not unheard of for them to travel together. So, without resting, they skinned it and then kept moving forward through the thick growth where there used to be a trail. It was no longer in use because the wildcats had become overpopulated and dangerous. Elkanah also knew that this was quite a shortcut into the back of his mother's village, in spite of it being a common, and dangerous zone for the Lynxes.

Later that afternoon, she could feel a chill in the air and was grateful for the fur Elkanah had given to her; she loosely tossed it over her shoulders and kept trudging along. It was most tiresome as they walked along in silence, but she was also thankful she had the durable moccasins the old woman had given to her.

They used their clubs to beat down a barrier of some high bushes and vines that was almost impenetrable, but not entirely. They kept moving forward and they finally reached a clearing on the other side of the high growth of bushes. They were just past some palmetto bushes when Danica heard the horrifying rattle that almost sounded like a hiss. She recognized it immediately as a Rattlesnake that was so common to Florida. It was coiled and ready to strike Elkanah. Before she could even open her mouth to warn him, he saw it just in time. When the snake struck at him, his powerful club whipped through the air, out from his side, as if chopping weeds or bushes.

The club struck the snake and knocked it back down to the ground. Elkanah drew his club back and out from his side again; he began to whip the snake each time it would draw back to strike at him. He knocked it to the ground again, and again until it was lifeless.

Danica stood frozen as she watched Elkanah remove the rattler from the snake's tail and put it into his pouch, and then he discarded the head by burying it. She quietly observed as he slit the snake open and cut up both sides of it, being careful to 'not cut' through the belly of the snake. Elkanah knew he would be able to trade the snakeskin, even the belly, for furs. He sliced the meat away from the skin and then he pulled a small pouch from within his larger pouch. It was filled with salt and he quickly salted the skin and rolled it up. Danica had seen this done before and knew that the salt was to keep insects from laying their larvae into the snakeskin. He placed the rolled-up skin into his pouch for later tanning.

"Hurry, help me build a fire," Elkanah told Danica. It didn't take long to start the fire and roast the snake. They hadn't eaten since they left the mission and they were pretty hungry.

"How do you know that there's no venom in the snake meat?" she asked, she seriously wanted to know.

"Because, the venom gland is in the head not the body, and remember, I buried that part. So, it's long gone," he said, trying to reassure her.

"Oh."

"If someone steps on the fang, even long after the snake is dead it can still have venom in it and kill you. That's why I buried it."

"I didn't know that." She made a face just thinking about it.

He handed her the first piece and she didn't hesitate to take a bite. "Not so bad," Danica said between bites.

They were deep in the forest by now and heard some hideous growls from furious creatures that Danica presumed were ravenous. Danica could not even imagine what they were and didn't even bother to ask. They just kept moving forward and soon it became obvious what these awful sounds were. Wild dogs had cornered a deer and were now furiously ripping it to pieces as they each fought to get their share.

The rain finally stopped again after another sudden downpour that soaked them to the bone, but eventually the sun came out drying things out a bit. Everything smelled so fresh and an earthy fragrance lingered in the air for a while.

They eventually reached a large river, and Elkanah seemed to know where he was going because they didn't cross it. They just walked along a well-traveled path near the river's edge. They soon came to a little area with a few people living in makeshift Lean-tos that did little to keep them dry when it rained, and even less to shelter them from the cooler weather that was soon to come.

Danica looked around and saw beaver pelts hanging from a couple of low hanging tree branches and more pelts were draped over a huge stump.

She was tired, so without anyone offering her a seat or hospitality, she found a cleared spot under a tree to rest her aching feet. Elkanah made his way over to several men that were casually standing around showing off their animal furs. Elkanah stretched out the snakeskin that appeared to be at least 9 feet in length. Danica curiously watched as they stretched the snakeskin out even more to inspect it. Interestingly, one of the other men handed Elkanah a beautiful, tawny wolf pelt in exchange for the skin.

A nasty looking man with snarly hair came over to Danica and tried to touch her leg. "What kind of person are you?" He reached out and pulled hard on her top trying to get a look to see what she had there.

"Get away!" She brushed his hand away in disgust.

When he tried to grab her inner thigh, she grabbed his cadaverous looking fingers in her hand and twisted until he let out a yell. All this did was piss him off and he came at her again trying to touch between her legs. She grabbed his snarled hair this time and wrapped it around her fingers and pulled his face down and in closer to hers. "Come over here and let me kick your ass, then you'll know what kind of person I am."

Still sitting, Danica pulled her skinning knife from the sheath inside her left moccasin and with a hard thrust, she aimed for his testicles. Skillfully she moved the knife up and along his thighs and towards his nuts and ass; she didn't care which, maybe she would slice both. She made a low guttural sound in her throat and with anger, she said in a deadly tone, "Better yet, maybe you should be a girl!" Her stony, cold eyes promised him that she would do it. She gave a hard push to let him know she was a fraction of an inch from penetrating his vulnerable ass or slicing his beloved penis open. *Yeah, maybe both*, she thought glaring at him contemplating her next move.

She was now eye-to-eye with him and her hostility was exceedingly clear. "Now try that again and I'll cut your asshole out! ASSHOLE!" There was now unmistakable fear in his bulging blue eyes and one eye looked like it might pop out of its socket. "Next time, I'll kill you. Now, get some manners."

Danica slipped her knife back into its sheath and then loosened her grip on his nasty hair. Without even thinking about it she couldn't help but slap him up beside the head. "You're so nasty." Danica said in the same low and deadly tone of voice to the offender, "And I don't know what stinks worse, your ass or your feet! Now move your stinking ass away from me." She could hear some muffled laughter behind her from the other hunters but she didn't care because she knew this pig deserved it.

About that time, she saw Elkanah walk up with an amused look in his eyes again. He leaned over and spoke to the visibly frightened man. "You'd better leave her alone, she'll do it. I meant to tell you about her, but I guess I don't have to now." And to Danica he said, "Ready to go? The raft man will take us to the other side."

They carefully stepped onto the raft and had to stand as the raft man moved the raft out and away from the shore with his long pole. The raft man had witnessed the incident and was laughing and making jokes about it as he skillfully moved them across the river. He was a friendly sort of guy with no teeth in the front and of slender build. Danica welcomed his cheerfulness after the encounter she had had with the filthy man they were all now referring to as 'Assfeet'.

Once on the other side of the river, it didn't take long to get to Elkanah's mother's village. As they were approaching the outer edges of the village, they could see someone leisurely moving about near a stream. When they got closer, Elkanah greeted the other person, and then said to Danica, "This is Moses, one of the other guides I was telling you about. He beat us here."

Moses seemed friendly enough and waved his hand to say 'hello'.

Elkanah explained to Danica, "He will travel with us, and is very useful and knowledgeable about the terrain north of here."

Danica couldn't help but notice the two scars that Moses had on his left arm, near his wrist and they appeared to be from knife wounds. Several larger scars were on his bare back near his left shoulder blade. It was clear that he had been bathing and she could clearly see that he was also of mixed blood, about 5'8", thick set and had many tattoos. His dark hair, thin and straight was quite long and Danica guessed that it was normally worn in a top knot that seemed to be so common among these dignified people.

CHAPTER 11

Elkanah led her into the enormous, circular Timucuan Village where his mother lived and through swarms of young warriors just waiting for their leader to instruct them on when and who to attack next; most notably Chua and his warriors. There was a lot of excitement and chatter among these warriors as they prepared their weapons for the next confrontation with enemy tribes. Some of the arrowheads they were carving were large and sharp, while others were small but sure to kill the intended target.

As they moved along, it was Danica's assessment that there were at least 5,000 young warriors in this village alone. It was huge and there was a lot of activity going on inside this village, more so than the other village she had visited before. They passed sights that were even more impressive, and she could see that this village alone was three times larger than the other village where she had danced and became a part of them.

Happy children also played here. They were mostly naked, but they didn't seem to realize that or care. Women carried baskets of fruits and vegetables, while others carried babies. Furs were hanging from skillfully made racks for drying, and at the back of the village, some men were carving out canoes and didn't even look up as Danica and Elkanah passed them by. Others were painting extraordinary patterns and designs onto their finished canoes, and another was putting a tattoo onto the shoulder of a happy young boy. This was for all to see what an enterprising young boy he was, and it was his reward for his feat of courage.

As they passed by this sight, she wondered if Elkanah had gotten his first tattoo that young. As if he was reading her mind, he said, "Some young boys get tattoos even younger than this one. Some girls too."

"How does that happen?"

"When they do something brave or spectacular, they will receive the greatly desired and envied tattoo. Do you see that Lynx there beside him? He killed it."

That answered it for Danica about why tattoos covered Elkanah's body. It told her a lot about him, and most of it she had already come to realize. She didn't say anything more about it because she didn't want him to know that she had seen his tattoos while he was bathing.

They came to a uniquely carved pole that stood at least 12 feet tall and it had an intricately carved face of an animal near the top. It was unexpectedly colorful and Danica noticed that at the very top of it, there was a bird with outstretched wings. It was a lot like her pendant that she had found by the river the day she was out canoeing with Josh. The bird was breathtaking. She casually took the bird out of her pocket to compare it to the bird at the top of the pole. *Not exactly the same,* she thought, *but close* and wondered again who lost it and what he was like.

Other colorful murals depicted life in this amazing village. Smaller poles lined an entrance to a hut of considerable size that had much activity and many warriors impressively posted around it. They seemed to have one purpose only, and that was to protect their highly esteemed leader.

As they came near the large hut, a tall, slender queen with a vibrant blue headdress had come out to welcome the two tired travelers even before they reached her hut. Word had already come to her of Elkanah's return. Danica felt a little confused to see such a greeting and didn't know what to expect next. Why would the queen be so eager to greet them?

The answer came soon enough when the queen greeted them both with a lot of enthusiasm. Much to Danica's surprise, the queen stretched her hand out affectionately towards Elkanah. "My warrior son has returned, welcome back."

"Mother." His eyes lit up when he saw her and took her hand into his hand. She led them both inside and after the happy reunion, he reached into his pouch and brought out the excellent wolf pelt for her to see. "I thought you would like this."

Queen Sushaney's smile showed her pleasure as she stroked the tawny pelt and commented on the remarkable beauty of the golden and brown colors that had waves of black and white. "It's truly a beautiful thing."

Danica was surprised at the gracefulness of the queen. She had two thick, black stripes tattooed into her skin from the right side of her forehead down to her chin and one stripe covered her eye. Even so, Danica could still see her delicate loveliness.

Several rows of silver and gold beads elegantly decorated her neck, and both wrists had matching bracelets made out of the same type of beads. She had long black hair beneath her headdress. She had gold jewelry dangling from her ears, and Danica was quick to notice that she only had one single hole piercing in each ear.

There were many strings of gold beads attached to her waistband and they made a clicking sound each time she moved. The waistband had oval shaped flaps of soft buckskin all the way around her body. These flaps went halfway down her muscular thighs and below the flaps were extremely artistic and permanent tattoos. The same types of tattoos were on her strong arms. Below her knees, she also had a thick stripe going around her right leg and one also going around her right ankle above her almost bare feet. Her shoes were nothing more than the soles with crude laces, but somewhat attractive.

She had a short cape of animal fur that loosely draped over her body and revealed a soft orange top that exposed a thin section of midriff. More sparkling silver jewelry with glittering stones connected the right side of her top to the skirt leaving the left side bare—Danica had the fleeting thought that Jordan should see this cool style. The top barely covered her small breasts and revealed a large scar on her arm near her shoulder, and another smaller scar was visible near her jaw and that puzzled Danica.

Queen Sushaney turned to Danica and said, "I hope you will feel welcome here, and I see that my son has safely brought you through the dangerous forest. I've heard about your grave situation and we wish to make you comfortable, and then we will talk about helping you get back to your place in life." She then led them inside another room of the extensive hut where several young women immediately assisted Danica in making her welcome and relaxed. Two more women came into the hut with fruit and another brought delicious smelling corn, beans and squash.

After resting there for a while, and after much conversation, Elkanah escorted her to another hut of her own to rest before the night's festivities.

There were many torches and fires throughout the village and she was keenly observant as they walked towards her hut. "Get a load of the point on that arrow!" She was amazed to see one warrior sharpening his large arrows of extremely heavy and thick stone. She openly stared as he filed each one to a terrifying and death-dealing point. She also observed some other large types of arrowheads and weapons made out of stone and rock that made a shiver go up her spine. She wasn't quite sure if she was shivering from fear or excitement, maybe both.

"Yes, the fine point will penetrate and split open the metal of the conquistador's armor. I'll get you some before we leave here, but be careful with them because he puts snake venom on the tips of the arrows," Elkanah said. "We are hearing that there is much trouble ahead from these conquistadors. Some are saying that they are now attacking with much fire coming out of their fingers,"

She nodded. "That's right. They will come with guns."

"What do you mean?" He stopped and turned to look at her in surprise. "How would you know this?"

"Where I come from, we have guns."

He nodded. "Do you mean trade guns that some warriors are getting from the Europeans?"

"Yes, sorta like that. Some are large and then there are handguns that you hold in your hand. See, like this." She held her arm straight out from her side as if aiming a small weapon at a target. "Or, like this." She gripped both hands together in front of her as if holding her 38 Special. "So, yeah, I guess it could look like fire coming out of their fingers, and if you have the opportunity to get trade guns, you should get all you can."

Danica didn't have the heart at this point to tell him the ending to this story, about how most of his people will be annihilated in the next couple of hundred years by these firearms. It was heart wrenching for her to think about it. She saw many questions in his eyes, but how could she explain to him about the sickening dilemma that she was in and how she had somehow gone back in time to the year 1624. She didn't understand it; how could she expect him to understand that she had somehow come here from the year 2017.

She saw the troubled look in his eyes again. "It's not good for us, is it?"

She shook her head no. "It won't be good." Danica was relieved when they started walking again, hoping the gun conversation was ended. It was, he got it.

About that time, Elkanah motioned towards a person quickly approaching them. "This is another guide. Do you remember on the trail when I was telling you about him? We will be fortunate to have two extra guides instead of one."

The third guide appeared to be about forty-five years of age; a somewhat dark-complected man with squint eyes. Danica looked at Elkanah in surprise because the guide stooped a little when walking and had the appearance that one leg was a little shorter than the other. He too had a top knot with two crooked and bent feathers; they appeared to be Eagle feathers that were in bad need of replacing. His clothes were dusty and she wondered about this because of all the rain.

As if reading her mind, Elkanah leaned over closer to her and said, "His name is William, and don't be fooled by his appearance. He is quick and very able to survive and help us to survive. He knows several languages that will be useful to us. Besides that, he knows where Chua and his warriors are hiding out and can lead us to them."

"Wait here." Elkanah walked over to William.

She waited as they talked. Danica sized William up from head to toe still wondering if he was really a good choice for a guide.

They paused for a moment and Elkanah motioned for her to come over to them. "Show her," Elkanah said to William. He pulled a monstrous bear claw out of his pouch and held it out for Danica to see.

"No joke! That's some heck of a bear claw you have there."

"Yes, it's a trophy." William was putting it back into his pouch carefully as if it were a piece of china or something.

She clearly understood now why he was all disheveled and dusty. She decided that it must have been one hell of a fight with William the courageous winner and proud owner of the monstrous bear claw. Danica assumed that he had multiple tattoos covering his body too. He did have several on his neck and one on his face. It was small red and black dots making a circle on the left side of his face; what that meant she didn't know.

He was tall like Elkanah and again, also of mixed blood. Danica was quickly coming to realize that this was a useful trait for survival in this wilderness if one is to be a guide. They knew the terrain, and she realized that being of mixed blood they had an advantage because they were able to understand the languages of some natives, as well as whites and were accepted by most unless it was a warring tribe.

Elkanah and Danica continued to walk through the village and she noticed one of the young warriors carving out a mask. As they got closer, Danica had to smother a scream. To her horror, the young warrior had placed gazing human eyes into the wooden, carved out eye sockets of the mask he was working on for the festivities that night. Danica almost gagged; they were staring and the color of the eyes were hazel, her exact eye color. She looked at this distasteful scene with repulsion mixed with fascination.

"Are you okay?" Elkanah leaned in to her.

"Yeah. Yeah, I'll be okay. A trophy, no doubt."

"Yes, and I told you this wouldn't be easy," he said.

She felt a weakness go over her and she just wished she could rest for a while, but pushed forward bracing herself for more sights like this. Nothing else unusual happened, but they did pass something somewhat strange. A tree that had arrow heads embedded into small branches and the wood was growing firmly around the arrowheads. She pointed at it and said, "What the heck?"

"They will soon become arrows." Elkanah explained.

"How clever."

Elkanah nodded in agreement.

Her place to rest that night was much like that at the other village where she had danced with the warriors, but the smell of animal dung was strong in the air and she soon realized that her hut was near an enclosure that held a breed of exceptionally fine and heavy horses.

She found out later from Elkanah that the Spanish Conquistadors had brought in these horses for the armored cavalry and some would escape the Spaniards, or they were left wandering after battles. The natives would gather them for their own use, but had to keep them hidden for fear others would steal them and possibly eat them. They also kept the horses out of sight from others because the Spaniards had also forbidden the sale of horses to natives.

"It has also been rumored for a long time that our village here has a lot of gold, so we are frequently attacked, but there are no large amounts of gold here at all. Our worst enemy of all is the evil Chua. He is convinced that we have gold, and besides that he hates the ones of us who are of mixed blood." Elkanah explained why so much war. "Chua trades the gold to Spaniards for trade items."

The next morning, Elkanah took Danica back to consult with his mother some more about the difficult situation she was in, and then the conversation turned to the warring tribe north of them. Queen Sushaney was quick to say, "Without a doubt, you will be attacked by some of Chua's warriors on your way to find the lady from the stars. They are exceedingly hostile right now."

If Danica had wondered about this elegant beauty's capabilities of being a queen, the doubt soon left her. Queen Sushaney's unreadable countenance now turned to cold unfriendliness when she spoke of the warring tribe and their leader. The queen leaned in closer to

134

Elkanah and never took her dark eyes off him. She lowered her voice and in a deadly tone said, "When you encounter Chua and his warriors, kill them. All of them."

Elkanah nodded. His eyes were dark and cold now as he listened to the queen's instructions.

"Take horses, and when you come to my other Chiefdom north of us, I want you to find Tah-Yah-Kee. Take him and some of his warriors with you. Together, you will find and kill Chua and his warriors." She then turned to Danica and said, "First they killed my husband, and then my father." She turned her blazing, dark eyes back to Elkanah and said in a low and deadly tone of voice, "I want them dead, and most of all, I want Chua dead and left for the animals to eat." Again, she turned back to Danica. "Just be warned, you cannot reach this lady you are looking for without conflict from this tribe. You too must become a warrior or else you will die. Do you understand this?"

Danica nodded and then understood how the queen had come to have scars. Danica's palms were sweating and her heart was racing as she realized what this queen was telling her and the possible outcome.

Elkanah leaned back and said to Danica, "You can stay here in the safety of this village, or go forward. It's your choice."

"I'll go."

She saw a flicker of understanding in Queen Sushaney's eyes. "I knew you would."

Queen Sushaney's eyes were still blazing as she turned back to Elkanah and handed him something shiny. "This is for your protection; it will bring you back to me unharmed." It was a silver pendant similar to the one Danica had found that day on the riverbank with Josh, but not exact.

After much more conversation, they went into another room of the hut that was of considerable size and again she saw a large selection of fruits and vegetables of all kinds. The same two women from the day before brought in what looked like roast lizards, rats, snake and meat that she was pretty sure was wild hog. After the long journey, Danica was glad to get any food and hospitality.

After the huge feast, and when Danica was feeling more at ease with Queen Sushaney, she asked, "I'm just curious, is there also a king in this village?"

"Not now, my father was the king and now I am the queen." Queen Sushaney turned back to Elkanah, "Tell Tah-Yah-Kee that I want Chua's eyes. And from you I want his gold that he so arrogantly wears in his ears. I want to know for certain that the fool is dead and mutilated beyond all recognition."

Elkanah's cold, dark eyes were intently focused on Queen Sushaney as he nodded. "He will die for sure."

Later that night the sound of drums, gourd rattles, and flutes with their hypnotic beat permeated Danica's brain until finally, and after watching Elkanah dance with the men, she realized that she had an intense desire to be a part of it. There was a lot of activity going on with heated dancing, and she couldn't resist the urge to join the women's festivities. She danced until she was completely exhausted and then watched for a while until, and to her surprise and liking, three warriors came over to her and danced around her, completing this portion of the celebration. Afterwards, she was tattooed with two impressive images on her arms. One tattoo was for the alligator she had killed, and the other one was for the Cougar she had killed on the trail in the Cougar zone. *How cool can this be*, she thought as the three warriors silently inked her skin. It was painful and she instinctively wanted to react to the stinging sensation, but she was determined to not flinch.

After the tattoos, the festivities were still not over. Fires flickered and many more warriors with their heads ornamented with great plumes of feathers appeared from nowhere until thousands of warriors were everywhere and looking especially frightful at night by the warm glows of the many fires. The energy in the air was electric, and Danica could hear and feel the excitement mounting because she realized that they were ready for war.

CHAPTER 12

The next morning William and Moses seemed psyched up and ready to go. They were waiting for Elkanah and Danica at the front of the village with large horses from the enclosure she had seen the night before. She had not seen Moses since they came near the village the first day they were there; it was when he had apparently been bathing. His hair had been loose and flowing down to his waist; it was now up in a top knot, just as Danica thought it would be. He had silver elegantly displayed in his ears and about his neck. A headdress of red, blues, greens and white was now wrapped in a graceful and stylish manner around his top knot. He also had a raccoon tail dangling down the side of his headdress. Mainly; for the most part, red feathers graced this headdress and he looked proud and strong as he mounted his horse. William had refreshed feathers and buckskins too. He looked equally as strong and impressive as Moses. When Danica's eyes moved over the two scouts and then back to Elkanah, she secretly admired them all three with respect and warm approval.

It didn't take long for Danica to get used to riding the horse that William had waiting for her. The horse's name was Arrow, and it was strong and elegant with a thick mane and tail. She wondered if it could possibly be an Andalusian horse because of its breathtaking beauty. The animal's stunning brown color glistened in the morning sun, and it was apparent that it was well cared for and a prized possession of Queen Sushaney's.

They rode for several hours going north from the Queen's village before coming upon a grisly sight that was unspeakable. A cabin out in the middle of nowhere was still burning from a recent Indian attack and the family was nowhere in sight.

"Over here." Moses motioned for them to come to the far side of the cabin and out near a field of peas. It was sickening, disgusting, and violent. The slaughter of that family was far worse than Danica had ever seen or imagined she would ever see. A warring tribe had ruthlessly mutilated the mother and killed the children. It was apparent that they were trying to run for their lives when they came to a sudden and unexpected end. The intense trepidation must have been unbearable as they suffered and died. It was clear to her that the family had been dead for a while. The father was nowhere in sight but she assumed he was lying dead somewhere close by. It was too horrendous to think about.

The mother's eye sockets where her eyeballs used to be were now showing bare bone. A hard blow under her eye had crushed the bones around her left eye before the removal of her eyes. Danica gagged at the sight of dried blood around her torn and violated vagina. Danica remembered the young warrior's mask with human eyes and trembled convulsively at this sight.

She saw that one single arrow had mercifully killed each of the children and they were not mutilated. Not more than five yards away was her husband lying face down and dead with his skull crushed. She felt darkness closing in and her trembling body was too weak to go forward.

"Don't look." Elkanah quickly dismounted and took Danica up into his arms and onto his horse with him, just like one would a child. And, also like a child, she buried her face into his chest blocking out all sights of the atrocities. His strong arms pulled her close to him and he held her tight to his chest without a word until they were long past the gruesome sight. When her trembling finally stopped, he loosened his hold on her a little and without a word, Moses handed the reins of her horse back to her.

Shortly down the path, a single Indian that was on foot approached them with a ferocious aggressiveness. He had a little bird claw for an earring and nothing in the other ear. A single sheaf of feathers came straight out of the knot of hair at the back of his head making him look like a hawk that was too muscular and strong to be argued with. She also noticed that he had a rather large and curved nose with a menacing long and slender face. However, his face did turn friendly when he saw them, and it was clear that Elkanah wanted him to join them. His club at his waist had signs of much use and small residues of flesh and hair that made her blood run cold. A rancid odor was offensively in the air and she felt nauseous as she realized that it was from fresh use. Elkanah didn't seem to notice, so she thought it best to ignore it as if she didn't notice it either.

Elkanah turned to Danica and said, "This is Tah-Yah-Kee, the brother to my mother, he will join us now."

She nodded her head towards him and said, "Hello."

Tah-Yah-Kee's piercing eyes were fastened on Danica and he nodded. "I've heard about your perplexing problem."

She wondered how word could have spread so quickly among these people, but she brushed that thought aside right away. She realized that they had their own way of spreading their news, and they were clearly expecting the arrival of Elkanah.

Danica wondered if Tah-Yah-Kee was incapable of emotion, but then she remembered his friendly demeanor when he had greeted Elkanah. She decided that all must be okay with him.

A few other Indians came into clear view now and had apparently been lingering just ahead and out of sight. They were around a bend in the path that sharply turned to the left and were among Live Oaks that were draped in moss. They were resting and waiting there for Tah-Yah-Kee in the shade of these inviting trees.

William and Moses had gone on ahead and were now casually interacting with them and it was clear that they were all comfortable with each other. It was becoming apparent to Danica that Tah-Yah-Kee was their leader. They all had that same aggressive demeanor that Tah-Yah-Kee had, but they spoke in their native tongue, unlike

Tah-Yah-Kee and Elkanah. They were speaking in English for Danica's benefit.

"Chua has done much harm to our village and to settlers in this area. He has been terrorizing the women and children up north of us by capturing and torturing them. He violently tears their flesh like a crazy animal would, but we will be done with him for good this time." Tah-Yah-Kee said with much disgust and hatred.

Elkanah intently listened to all that Tah-Yah-Kee had to say about Chua and his rampages. And now, Danica completely understood the dark and dreaded looks that Elkanah displayed. His fury was about to be unleashed on Chua and his warriors for the death of his father and then his grandfather.

"I will kill him myself; this I promise." Elkanah said in a cold voice.

Danica felt a flow of energy surge through her as she intently listened to every plan they discussed, and the most interesting part of all was the surprise attack they had planned for Chua and his warriors. Tah-Yah-Kee already knew that Chua and his warriors outnumbered them, so they planned to slip up on them in the middle of the night and attack. Without a doubt, in the middle of the dark forest where Chua was camped, would be the tragic demise and final burial grounds for him. Danica decided that the ingenuity of it all was incredible and would probably work.

Excitement filled every fiber of her being. She wanted to be a part of the attack and was in complete agreement with them. To her surprise, they continued to speak in English to include her in all their plans.

Tah-Yah-Kee led the way and they soon approached a small village that was not too far up the path. To her relief, they made her welcome there by offering necessities, and a place to rest the horses. Danica and the others rested there for one day and night waiting for a few more reinforcement braves to join them from another village. That night there was more feasting and celebrations. Food much like that at the other villages. Deer, fish, boiled corn, peas, squash, a pot with sweet berries and what looked like dumplings that was served in wooden trays and with wooden spoons by muscular women. Some young, some not so young. They were pleasant and brought Danica some Casseena (yaupon tea), a ritual tea that she consumed in small amounts not sure of the effect it would have on her.

After the other warriors arrived, they didn't feel the need to linger there any longer than necessary. However, they did have to leave the horses there because the terrain ahead was too rough for the horses, and they knew they would have to travel quite a distance by raft to reach the other mission.

They soon crossed a small lake and then came to a field that seemed to go on forever. Elkanah was observing the territory. "We have to run across this field without stopping before the dust worms come out to feed. They eat everything in their path."

"Really? Dust worms?" She said in wide-eyed amazement.

"Yes, are you ready?"

"Yeah, let's do it." They all ran as fast as they could, but they didn't quite make it to the other side before giant dust worms came out of nowhere. The giant dust worms moved back and forth eating palmettos, unlucky birds that were sleeping in vegetation, reeds along the edge of the field, and anything in their path. Danica felt like screaming when she heard the sound of birds squawking as they became a meal for a dust worm.

Once past that commotion they were able to rest a little beside a stream. "I've heard of a giant armadillo before, but never giant dust worms. Dang!" Danica shook her head in disbelief. "Whew-and I thought I'd seen it all."

"You've never seen a dust worm before?" Elkanah seemed surprised.

"Not ever." She shook her head in disbelief. "Never even heard of them."

Moses held his hand up for silence and Danica now understood the reason for this. She had learned from her experience in the trees to listen for every sound and to pick up on the smells of animals that could be nearby. Crickets would even quit chirping when they detected danger nearby.

Moses quietly moved out and away from the others and off into the woods in search of food. They didn't have to wait very long

144

because Moses soon came walking back carrying two large rabbits. Tah-Yah-Kee's warriors had already spread out for the night to guard the territory. Danica saw that they hunted for their own food and had amazingly killed a large deer. It was prepared without delay and cut into several large pieces. A warrior brought Moses a large slice and he placed it on one of the fires that were scattered about the camping area. They all casually mingled about and talked in low tones about how they would go about finding Chua. He was not to be captured, but killed on the spot.

"Pretty good," Danica said after they had roasted the rabbits and deer over the hot fires.

"Let's rest here for the night because there is rougher terrain ahead, and then we will head towards the beach." William decided. "At least here, we can fish in the morning, and we already have warm fires."

"Are you sure? I would still continue north." Moses contradicted William.

William sharply rebuked him as if offended. "Go your way then, and you'll go straight to your death. I've already heard that this way is blocked with many of our enemy that have reassembled and joined forces with some Spaniards to war against us. We are too outnumbered to go this way. We will go west, then around them, and then like a fox we will find Chua and kill him. We have a chance if we encounter a small number of enemies, but we will all die if we go north."

Danica quietly watched the dispute and Elkanah leaned over and whispered in her ear, "This is an insult to William if you question his judgment. This is not good, and besides that, William is right and we have to find and kill Chua. Without their leader, they will feel great confusion and weakness."

She nodded, attentively listening.

It turned a little cool that night, but the fur Elkanah had given to her was unbelievably warm along with the flickering fires, that to her amazement, didn't go out. And almost to Danica's embarrassment, that was mingled with pleasure, she kept waking up throughout the night dreaming of Elkanah taking her into his strong, but gentle arms, just like he did on horseback. She could still feel the way he cradled her in his arms, and the scent of him still lingered with her. She remembered the way her cheek had rested on his chest, and in her dreams, he stroked her bare breasts and then bedded her that very night. It was strange and tender, but almost animal like. She liked it.

The next morning, they had fish roasted over the fire that was still burning. Danica curiously watched as Moses speared several fish that had retreated to a pool, in the shallow stream. She almost found it entertaining the way he would spear a fish, and then pull it back with some vines that had been tied around his spear. He caught several fish this way, and soon had them cooking in the stone oven he had made out of stacked, flat rocks. He wrapped the fish in some non-poisonous leaves that she suspected were banana leaves and tied

146

them like bundles, with safe vines. *Interesting* is all she could think, and they were delicious and flavorful.

It was a beautiful morning and she found a grassy spot near a tree to sit and just relax before they were all ready to go. The sunlight was beginning to glitter through the trees and it felt good after all the rain. And then, without warning, Elkanah came over and sat down beside her. She drew back a little and her heart raced when he accidentally brushed up against her shoulder as he was sitting down. He came so close to her that she could feel the warmth of his body, and this alarmed her because his touch was so pleasant. She heard a slight rustling and scraping sound when feathers in his headdress rubbed together, and the smell of leather was a good smell as he lowered his large body to the ground beside her. She felt mixed feelings of fear and excitement, and then confusion because he was so different from Alex. Her thoughts went back to the day in the canoe when his moccasin accidently touched her face and the fear that surged through her. And then her thoughts went to the day on horseback when his arms were wrapped tightly around her keeping her safe. She secretly wanted to feel his strong arms around her again.

"I just wanted you to know what to expect. Today we will head towards the beaches and there we could possibly have confrontations with some of the pirates that have docked there. We'll try to avoid confrontation by staying near the edge of the woods. However, if we should encounter them, try to stay out of their way. Okay?"

She felt that his dark eyes could see into her thoughts and into her dreams where he had bedded her, so she quickly looked away. "Okay," she said.

He leaned in closer and she was forced to look back at him and couldn't help but notice the curve of his mouth, the way his upper lip dipped down in the middle. "If you can't stay out of their way, fight with everything you have within you. Okay?"

"Okay."

"And Danica, you really don't have to be afraid of me."

"I'm not."

"Is that why you flinch when I come near you?"

"No." She didn't know how to answer that one.

"Well, I'm just trying to tell you something. I promised you that first day we left that I'm not going to do anything to you. And I'm also trying to tell you that I…

About that time, they saw Tah-Yah-Kee and some of his warriors moving on out, and away from their campsite to walk ahead of them, and then she saw more of the warriors lingering behind so they could walk behind her and Elkanah. That was a comforting sight to Danica.

"Ready?" Elkanah said.

"Ready."

CHAPTER 13

It happened down by the beach when the pirates swarmed them with guns and swords. They were a ragged looking crew with a mixture of castaways of many nationalities. Some stray displaced Spanish conquistadors, some starving survivors of shipwrecks that necessitated a dreaded decision to join the pirates. Some were just greedy for gold and silver, and others were looking for adventure.

She didn't know where they came from, but she hid herself behind some tall bushes, but not in time. In a horrified fascination, she watched and counted at least three Spanish galleons that were anchored there in the bay and clearly taken over by pirates. The largest one was at least one hundred feet long and thirty feet wide. It had four masts and three decks that displayed innumerable cannons ready to take action as if they were the true kings of the sea. Many people moved about, doing this and that, but most threatening to Danica was the Conquistadors she saw milling around as if waiting for orders. She felt sick to her stomach at the realization that they were at least three times outnumbered by these pirates that had taken over these (for whatever reasons) disadvantaged Spaniards. She knew that disastrous events had befallen many of them at some point in time, but still, she realized that they were now very dangerous men. It gradually sunk in that *she was in deep trouble* and she just wanted to go home, *but this was the way home*, around these people.

She surmised that the largest ship had been the galleon of the Captain General and carried the crown's silver. *Incredible*, Danica's mouth moved, but no sound came out. She stayed crouched down in a small ball and continued to scrutinize the other galleons. Next to the largest one was a smaller ship, but still impressive and heavily armed with cannons. *Wow*, she mouthed again. She remembered from her history class that the heavily armed ships carried the most silver from Peru, and she decided that, without a doubt, this one was the galleon of the Admiral before the pirates took over.

She saw another unarmed galleon and assumed it carried cargo, tools, domestic animals, and passengers. To her regret she saw numerous smaller boats called *pataches* that were moving between the larger galleons, doing what, she didn't know. But she didn't quite trust this situation because she also knew these smaller vessels were used for surveillance and they were inspecting all along the coasts. Some were anchored and this made her even more uneasy as she realized some might be on the beach by now inspecting the territory.

She watched in horror while three small boats made their way in closer to shore and stopped short of a shallow sand bar. Once anchored, many pirates that were mingled in with conquistadors, jumped quickly from the small boats. Some were shouting and cursing, and some were speaking in foreign languages that she did not understand.

They were moving around some mangroves and swarmed the beaches in every direction searching for any signs of life. Her heart filled with terror as they aggressively came closer, and closer until they made their way in even closer to where she was hiding. Two more small boats filled with unruly pirates came in and swarmed the beaches and sand dunes. They trampled down sea oats and brushed past palmettos that were growing freely around sabal palms and bushes. As they moved in closer, she was aware of her own breathing and tried to not make a sound as they frighteningly swooshed past her where she was crouched down and hiding. They came so close to the palmettos and bushes where she was hiding that she almost gagged from the smell of dirty bodies and rum.

A small scream tore out of her throat as huge hands smashed down on the back of her neck slamming her to the sandy beach. The monstrous hands held her captive as the huge *'thing'* jerked her back up by the back of her hair and then slammed her face down into the white sand, again and again. She was keenly aware of the gritty texture of the sand under her hands and in her mouth and face; she was powerless to defend herself.

She was vaguely aware of her surroundings and all that went through her mind was that *'this thing'* was slinging her around like a rag doll. The stink from the *'thing'* attacking her was putrid and he was making grunting noises that totally freaked her out. It made her want to gag as he covered her body with his body making his intentions clear. He ripped at her clothes trying to tear them off. Danica heard a dull thwack followed by a thud and the *'thing'* fell off her and onto the ground. The *'thing'* had a club sticking out of the side of his face beside his ear. With an angry jerk, Elkanah pulled his club out of the pirate's face and blood spattered everywhere as he buried it again, and again until he was sure the attacker was dead. Blood flowed into the white beach sand and a brief salty breeze was a blessed relief from the rot stench of the attacker.

Elkanah reached for Danica and lifted her up and into his safe arms. He held her tight to him and ran towards some palmettos on the edge of some woods.

"Get behind those palmettos and thickets over there at the edge of the woods and stay there." Elkanah ordered Danica. Arrows were flying all around her as Elkanah and the other warriors fearlessly fought their enemies. Bodies dropped like flies. A wave of fearsome sounds filled the thick air as the warriors, over and over, swarmed back at the pirates. Danica knew she was on her own as she braced herself for the worst. It came; it wasn't over. Still another swarm of pirates and Spaniards rushed them coming from two more small boats and then onto the beach. They came extremely close to where Danica was hiding behind a dense group of bushes and trees.

The swift movement of their cross bows terrified her. This time Danica had no choice as she quickly reached for her bow and one of the monstrous arrows that Elkanah had given to her at his mother's village. She carefully and deliberately pulled her bow back and took aim at a howling attacker as he turned his ferocious attention towards her. She felt empowered as her arrow pierced his armor and brought him down to the white sand. Fearlessly, she joined the massacre and smashed another in the face with her club. She felt the air from something moving swiftly past her head and realized that by luck, she had turned in time to dodge an arrow. With an angry shriek, she struck another attacker down with another deadly face blow from her club.

She braced herself for the next enemy to come at her, but there was nothing but an abnormal stillness all around her even though the haunting sounds of blood curdling screams and bashing was still close by.

Cautiously, she peered in every direction and just stood there on guard for a few minutes. When all seemed clear, Danica got out of sight by getting back behind the palmettos to wait for the next attack that was sure to come. She noticed a small trail that led into some heavier woods nearby. She quickly ran down that trail in search of anything that she could use to make a primitive booby trap. She was in luck and saw a dirty looking mud puddle and remembered her grandpa's stories about badass camouflage. She quickly smeared some light-colored mud onto her face and then smeared splotches of the dirtier mud over that. She repeated this until her whole face, hair, and hands were covered. She then covered her clothes with mud and made a mental note to rip a piece of fabric from a corpse to tie over her moccasins so she wouldn't leave any footprints.

This time she saw where they were coming from, but they didn't see her. The booby traps seemed to be the natural thing to do as she devised her plan to ambush as many as possible.

After her time spent in the trees, Danica knew which of the vines were strong enough to use for a booby trap. She chose vines that wouldn't break and could be used to trip her assailants and ambush them. The vine would then become the lethal weapon that her strong hands would use to squeeze the life out of the attacker. It was primitive, but she knew it would work. She took her colorful top off and placed it over a limb on the other side of the path because she knew this would attract the enemy's attention. The slight breeze created movement and the tunic gently moved back and forth making it look like a person moving around. She also placed a brightly painted arrow nearby to divert attention. Then she waited.

One by one, she killed many that day and moved them out of sight until there was no further movement.

It was finally over. She could tell by the sinister quietness in the air and it was nauseatingly still. Suddenly, she heard someone moving through the bushes, twigs snapped and then she saw the top of Elkanah's head. The headdress was long gone and his top knot was messy and tangled strings of hair trailed down around his face. He was sweaty, battle weary and disheveled.

"Elkanah, over here!" She was utterly exhausted.

"What's this?" He was amazed at her cleverly created booby trap.

"It's a booby trap. I learned it in the military, and from my grandfather," she said without hesitation.

The intensity and the ferocity of his gaze seemed to pierce through to her very soul as he realized her shrewdness.

"You told me to stay here, so I did. But, not at first, and then I wondered what my grandpa would tell me to do. So, I figured he would tell me to do this." She motioned towards her face and body and then towards her extremely basic booby trap. She then showed him the bodies she had pulled out of sight during the ambush.

"Yes, I see. You are good to have around." He shook his head in amazement and quietly scrutinized the situation.

"Where are the others?" Danica asked.

"Not sure, I was looking for you. Let's go see where they are."

They saw a dazed Tah-Yah-Kee first and knew instantly that he didn't have good news. Several warriors had lost their lives that day, and shortly Moses and William made their way to them. Moses had numerous cuts about his face and neck; some gashes were deep and bleeding. Danica had learned to always keep at least one piece of aloe and cattail in her cargo pants for emergencies. She quickly broke the cattail into pieces and placed a piece on each of his deeper cuts in hopes that it would stop the bleeding.

They surveyed the damage done and saw that they had killed an innumerable amount of attackers along with many of Chua's warriors who had sided up with the pirates for added strength, and no doubt silver and gold. Unfortunately, Chua and a few of his warriors had managed to escape.

They felt that it would be wise to move on down the beach and away from the battle site just in case other enemies should appear. They found a good resting place with nice sabal palms to relax under where Danica helped Moses clean his wounds a little better. Plantain plants were plentiful, so she made a poultice of water and crushed plantain leaves to put on each of his cuts in hopes it would keep down infection and pain.

After some much-needed rest, Elkanah, William and Moses laid out the plan to wait until nightfall, and then they would find Chua and kill him by night, when he least expected it.

William had suggested, "If we move by night, we can let the stars guide us to where Chua is hiding."

Elkanah nodded.

Danica noticed that William and Moses were now in complete agreement on the action they should take to find the much-hated Chua. They had moved on down the beach, a few feet away from Danica, but she could still hear muffled conversation as they plotted to find and kill Chua.

As soon as it was dark, they set out to find the loathsome Chua. Without hesitation, William and Moses led the way and Danica realized this one important thing about them both. That in spite of their differences, they had this one powerful bond - they completely trusted each other in the face of death. And it became clear to Danica that they both had the ability to move quickly and easily through the thick patches of entangled trees and vines, and William was certain he knew the whereabouts of Chua. Elkanah and Danica were a few paces behind them, and Tah-Yah-Kee and most of his warriors had scattered out behind them. A few were up front with William and Moses. They moved steadfastly into the coal black forest and could barely make out the way before them until their eyes adjusted to the dark.

They quietly walked for about an hour or so and then sudden movement ahead caught the attention of Moses and William. Moses motioned for Elkanah and Danica to get down. They all four threw themselves down behind some trees and curled up so the passing men would not see them. Some of the passing men were warriors of Chua's with a few stray Spaniards that had joined their forces. Once Chua's men had passed them, the four got up and closed in on the enemy knowing that Tah-Yah-Kee and his warriors were scattered out in the woods around and behind them. At the right moment they would all close in on them, totally surrounding the enemy. Chua's men walked into a quick and brutal death.

Tah-Yah-Kee and his warriors seemed even more electrically charged now than before, and ready to finish the battle. And now, with even more persistence, they continued to move in closer to where Chua was sure to be hiding. The energy was high as they all quietly made their way through the thick forest and to the camp of Chua. Danica had the fleeting thought that *it was too late to opt out of this plan.*

They knew they were getting close because of the smell of smoke that was coming from the nearby camp. The closer they got to the camp, the attitude of Tah-Yah-Kee and his warriors was one of more pronounced hostility. Finally, they saw them, but they heard them first. Three were a little disagreeable and harsh sounding towards one another, while another group of warriors was standing alone speaking in low tones. Some were standing and moving about, and others were just sitting. *Creepy,* Danica thought, because their faces looked hideous with the campfire below them and the flickering fire coming up around their faces made them look unnatural and as dangerous as she knew they were.

Elkanah finally gave the signal to attack, and Chua and his warriors were justifiably caught off guard. William and Moses rushed in and fought tirelessly. They killed warrior after warrior. They held back the enemy as Tah-Yah-Kee and Elkanah moved in to find and finish the job of killing Chua.

The sickening thuds – the screams – the sound of heavy clubs making contact with skulls resonated through the night, and past

Danica's ears as she fought savagely and without fear knowing that she would die here in this dark and gruesome wilderness if she didn't fight back with all of her might. Tah-Yah-Kee and his warriors ripped and mauled many in their search for Chua, and Danica stepped over and around the already putrid smelling bodies. Thud after thud vibrated, and kept vibrating, and vibrating, and vibrating through Danica's hearing to her brain and left her feeling nothing but numb, so she kept killing to stay alive. As each chilling cry continued to reverberate across the damp forest and into her ears, it was telling her that Tah-Yah-Kee and Elkanah were moving in closer to Chua.

Suddenly, under the eerie shadows of the moon, Chua was there and this was the first sight Danica had gotten of him up close. His body was bare from the waist up and his muscular, tattooed body was big. His face was twisted into an ugly scowl and he had many strands of leather with beads trailing down the sides and back of his head from a tight top knot. From this top knot were short, red feathers attached close together at the base and spread out around the back of his head. He was evil in the flesh.

He walked towards them with a stiff, erect, and apparently pompous strut and stopped just short of being in Elkanah's face. He spit at Elkanah, and with a blood-chilling shout, Elkanah charged at him. He brought the first blow to Chua with his club. Blood and sweat splattered in all directions and Danica watched in horror as Chua staggered a little and then regained his strength. She stood frozen in the moment to see these two powerfully built men struggle to gain the advantage over the other. Chua swung at Elkanah with his club and it grazed off his arm, but then Danica saw blood coming from the gash and knew that it was deep. Rage flared up in Elkanah and his next blow to Chua brought him to the ground. It gave Elkanah the advantage, but for one long and freakish moment Chua's eyes met Danica's and this chilled her to the bone. In a flash, Elkanah plunged the club deep into Chua's skull and a haunting gurgle came from his throat. She watched without feelings as Elkanah plunged the club into Chua again, and again until he knew for certain he was dead.

"Today was your day to die Chua! You die for my father and my grandfather," Elkanah said, and then his spear went through Chua as if claiming victory. Danica stared in disbelief as Elkanah sliced Chua's right ear off and then his left – the ears that so arrogantly displayed the prized ear jewelry that Queen Sushaney had demanded.

Danica still stood frozen as Tah-Yah-Kee gouged Chua's vacant and staring eyes out. Tah-Yah-Kee let out a fierce scream, "And for the many women and children from my village that you so viciously slaughtered."

Some of the warriors sickeningly cut out Chua's liver and ate it. Danica didn't even look away when they dismembered him and victoriously inserted a spear up his ass. She only turned away when Elkanah said, "Hurry, let's check out the rest of the encampment."

Without hesitation, they searched the small encampment of Chua's and what they did find astonished them both. They found two white girls tied up near the back of the camp. They appeared to be in their late teens and to Danica's amazement, they were wearing threadbare clothes. And, even more to her amazement, she recognized them as Irene and Charm, the two sisters from the posters she had seen still scattered about town before her canoeing accident. They had turned up missing late last year just a few months before Danica had returned home from the Army, and just like Danica, they had been canoeing with their friends. Their canoe had overturned and they were never found. It was assumed that the alligators had eaten them.

"Hurry!" Danica saw relief in the girl's eyes as she sliced the leather that was binding them at their wrists. "Come with us."

Again, Danica ordered, "Hurry, let's get outta here." Danica noticed that they were both weak, but they gladly followed. Danica also realized that they couldn't keep up with her, so she had to walk at a slower pace and she helped the weaker one along.

Charm, the younger, and the weaker of the two girls was crying. "We were raped so many times."

"You'll be okay now." Danica walked with her arm around her until she was calmed and they were a long distance from the encampment of Chua.

"Tell me about it. How did you get here?" Danica wasn't surprised to hear almost word for word, that the same exact thing that had

161

happened to her, had happened to them, except some of Chua's warriors immediately kidnapped the girls after their canoeing accident. They had no clue about what had happened to them concerning the blue rainbow. It just couldn't be explained.

CHAPTER 14

They didn't waste any time as they headed north by raft towards the other mission. The river was the only way to get there and they were eager to find Friar Simon. Elkanah and Danica went in first to talk to the friar. They briefly told him about the lady from the stars and Danica assured him that she seriously needed his help in finding her. She desperately wanted to go home.

Friar Simon knew exactly how they could get to her and gave explicit directions. "I've seen her face to face or else I wouldn't have believed it. First, you will need to find the gatekeeper to 'the lady' and her name is Nolia, the lizard woman. She is the one that actually knows where 'the lady' is and will tell you how to get to her. Nolia stays near the caverns, so she shouldn't be too hard to find, but just be careful."

"The lizard woman?" Danica arched an eyebrow at this comment while surreal images bounced through her mind.

"Yes, you will know her when you see her."

"Oh, okay."

"Please, make yourselves comfortable here and have your traveling companions come in and rest. I'll have refreshments in a while for you all."

"Thank you, but sir, I have two girls with us that are very weak. Do you think we can take care of their needs first?"

"Of course."

When the friar saw how weak Irene and Charm were, he assisted them himself. He quickly ushered them into the mission and made them comfortable by bringing hot tea. A few minutes later, he brought out hot oats with maple syrup and a large plate of bread. Shortly after that, another friar brought out more oats, but a larger pot this time and then he brought out cheese, butter, blackberry jam, and smoked ham for all. They were grateful for the kindness the friars offered.

Tah-Yah-Kee and his warriors had already spread out on their own and had a fire going to roast a pig they had speared outside the mission walls. Danica had already come to the realization that they had their own way of doing things and she didn't question it. She also knew that the friars would talk to Tah-Yah-Kee and his warriors about their souls, and they resisted that. However, Danica, Elkanah and the girls respectfully heard their teachings and prayers.

Later, the friar walked them out through a door with high arches, and out into a garden area that had benches and beautiful flowers scattered about. He took them out through a gate towards another building that had many people just standing around. Some were sitting on benches and then something caught Danica's attention. A woman wearing a long black dress, with a black lace scarf covering her head, was trying to deal with a whiny kid. Her dress was in a tattered condition with a lot of sandspurs stuck to the hem of her garment.

"Who are these people?" Danica couldn't contain her curiosity.

"Tragic. Just tragic," Friar Simon started out speaking with pity. "The poor souls are staying here a few days to rest, and then they will be leaving to go to another area to hopefully board a ship to Spain. And from there back to their own homelands.

"Why? What happened to them?"

About that time, the woman in the black dress yanked the kid up because he had sat down and refused to get up and walk. He was whining even louder.

"Several weeks back, a hurricane destroyed all five of their ships filled with provisions and they lost almost everything they owned." He spread his hands out. "Almost everything was totally destroyed."

"How sad, she said.

"Yes, they were going to start a new settlement west of here but they barely saved themselves. They're not very happy right now with their lot in life."

Danica shook her head and said, "I'm sorry about that", and continued to listen to the friar's story.

"Yes, so one day they all just came trudging in being led by their Captain-General. He did all he could to encourage them to keep traveling and sadly, some didn't make it. They had to leave graves behind and they were crying and praying. It was just heart wrenching to hear the crying.

"The weather was still bad when they got here and I just can't imagine how those ladies made it through the forest with those long skirts dripping wet. The Captain-General was a slight built man, but strong, so he helped them along all he could. They survived the high winds from the storm by hanging onto debris and they floated to shore in different places after their boats broke into pieces. He did show much concern for them and did his best to get them to us and to safety before he and several other men left to go back in search of other survivors."

Loud talking brought their attention back to the group of people, and it was obvious that someone was having a heated argument.

Friar Simon shook his head and reluctantly said, "I wouldn't go too near them though, and I hate to say this, but they are not a pleasant bunch. They are actually quite mean, and they fight a lot among themselves over the few provisions they were able to salvage."

"Too bad."

"See that one over there?" He pointed to a woman sitting alone near the gate.

Danica nodded.

"She bit one of the other women and her husband had to pull her off. She's not well liked. Anyway, they're all a brutish bunch and we'll be glad to see them go."

They were glad to move along and get past them to another area of the mission where they could rest for the night. There were small houses scattered in the edge of the woods beside the mission. The friar pointed and said, "There, over there is where you will stay tonight."

"Thank you." Elkanah expressed his appreciation to the friar.

"I am happy to be of help."

The next morning a young friar had breakfast ready for them before they set out for the caverns. He brought out fresh bread, honey, eggs, more oats and ham. The girls were obviously feeling a lot stronger after sleeping on a real bed and having warm food in their stomachs.

As they were leaving the mission, they met up with the friar again that had assisted them the day before. Danica thanked him again for their kindness and she mentioned to him how thoughtful the young friar was that brought out their breakfast.

"Yes, he is thoughtful, but it's such a pity though, because he will be going back with the others when their ship comes to rescue them." He leaned in closer to Danica then and lowered his voice as if ashamed. "He was discovered having an illicit relationship with the widow that wears the black clothing. The one with the young child."

167

"What?" Danica was truly shocked to hear this news.

"Yes, it is such a shame for him to go back in disgrace."

She just shook her head in disbelief.

"Yes, those people have no shame and have just been trouble for us here. We want to see them go. Anyway, when you get to the caverns you can just ask for Nolia and anybody can tell you where she is." He walked all the way out to see them off and to wish them well. Danica looked back once and he was still standing there outside the huge gate waving and watching them leave. She gave one last wave before he was completely out of sight.

"Did you hear what he said about the young friar?" She asked Elkanah and was still in disbelief.

"Yes, but I already thought so because of the way he kept looking at her and acting sheepish."

"What? You noticed."

"It was pretty obvious."

She just shook her head again.

After they left the mission, they traveled for about three miles and reached a pretty inlet that had scattered mangroves all along the coastline. As they approached, they heard faint sounds of crying coming from behind some large mangroves that were growing in shallow and clear water. The water appeared to be about knee deep, and not even that deep in some places. There had obviously been a ship wreck because of the scattered debris that had washed ashore. As they got closer, they heard male and female voices, some were sobbing and calling out to God in a pitiful way. They were clearly in anguish.

Danica moved on around the large area of mangrove trees that were temporarily shielding the frightened people from what they thought was more danger coming their way. They had seen Elkanah, William and Moses as they approached.

They were huddled together in the knee-deep water, amongst the tangled mangrove roots that grow in brackish water. Danica made first sight of them and thought, *not a very suitable place for them to hang out*. They were clearly terrified so Danica approached them first.

There were two very skinny men and three women who were also undernourished. "Hello." Danica raised her hand in a slight wave. They tried to back further away from her and were now pushing closer into the Mangroves and deeper into the water.

"Can we help you? Come on, let me help you." Danica reached her hand out to help them. The frailest of all the women took her hand and shakily stepped forward.

"Come on, you others need to let me help you too," Danica said. "You don't want to be in there with all those crabs. Just not a good place to be." Danica waited a minute and then offered again, "Come on, let's get you out of there." One at a time, the others let her help them until they were all out and in a safer place.

Elkanah saw that they were afraid of him so he stayed back until Danica motioned for him to come over.

"This is Elkanah. He is a guide and can help you get to a mission and to safety. So, what happened? How did you get here and where are you from?"

One of the skinny men understood Danica and stepped forward. "Most of us are from Spain and the others are from different places. There came a high wind that destroyed all five of our ships. We were attempting to colonize here but it didn't work out for us. Almost everything we own was destroyed and so many died." He paused a minute and looked down and then continued to tell his story. "Our ship was run aground and broke into pieces. Totally destroyed but we thought we might be able to salvage some things here in the water."

"We'll help you, but for now maybe you would like for us to make a fire so we can cook those crabs." She pointed to a lot of them around the mangrove roots.

"Yes, thank you. We would all appreciate that." He turned to the others and spoke to them in Spanish, assuring them that all would be well.

William and Moses had been staying back until the survivors had relaxed a bit. Tah-Yah-Kee and his warriors were staying back in the woods, just out of sight. They all knew that the survivors were suffering from a disturbingly deep trauma and grief over the loss of their loved ones, and they also lost most of their provisions. Slowly, so as not to upset the survivors, William and Moses came forward bringing bits of red meat, several wild turkeys and plantains to roast for the weary people.

Danica saw the skinny man's eyes widen in surprise and he drew back in mistrust.

Danica quickly said, "No need to worry. These are more guides that will help you back to the mission we left just a short while ago, but first, you all need some food. They have food for you. Try to rest a little and we'll help you salvage some things."

Elkanah stepped forward. "Also, when we get to the mission, we can have a few men come back with a cart to salvage what we can for you." Elkanah spoke again, "I also want to tell you that other survivors were also found, but pretty far from here. They are waiting at the mission for a ship to rescue them so they can return to Spain. I assume you want that too."

The skinny man looked surprised and inquisitive when he heard Elkanah speaking the English language with smoothness and confidence. Danica smiled and thought, *this guy definitely does not have a poker face.*

Danica went ahead and answered this for the skinny man, "His father was British and his mother is Timucuan. The same with William and Moses over there. No need to fear them; they will help you back to the mission and to safety."

"Oh, okay." He turned and passed on this information to the others in Spanish. Some cried and thanked God. They were visibly more relaxed after this assurance.

After they had eaten and rested for a while, Danica and Elkanah helped them salvage a few small items. The first thing they found was an ivory manicure set. They kept looking in the same spot and found a tortoise shell hair comb, an ivory comb with pearls, some ceramic plates, a nice piece of pottery, some large vessels holding olives, farming tools, a trunk with the name Sophia carved into the wood on the front of it. And then, much to their delight, they found wine and other supplies to include multi colored fabrics that was saturated and heavy with water and beach sand.

"We'll have someone come back for these larger items, but for now, let's head out for the mission," Elkanah said."

A short distance up the well-traveled path, Danica was walking ahead of Elkanah and heard a heart wrenching sound. It was a woman just sitting on the ground at the edge of a thick forest and she was crying uncontrollably.

"Quick." Danica called out to Elkanah, "Come over here. Here's another one."

"What is it?"

"Look, help me with this woman."

Danica hurried over to her and reached down to help her up. "Here, let me help you." Elkanah rushed to help her. Danica took one arm of the woman and Elkanah took the other. They gently lifted her to her feet. They didn't have to ask, it was obvious. She had been burying someone. She had a small shovel in her hand, and dropped it when they lifted her.

"Honey, can you tell me what happened," Danica said.

The woman spoke in a soft and sweet tone of voice, much like Fleur, and with a slight French accent. Between sobs she said, "We were trying to salvage some of our possessions and we got separated from the others, and then we couldn't find them. We had heard of another settlement in this direction and thought that they went there, but then we couldn't find that either. We had no bread left and thought that if we could reach that settlement in time, then we could get help, but we could find no one." She gave a dispirited little shrug, clearly in a lot of distress and depressed. "We had been told that at this other settlement we could wait for another ship to take us back home, but it might take up to 3 years for a ship to come into that port. We had decided that this was a mistake to be here and we wished to return to our own home. And then my husband started having severe stomach cramps and fever. He got too sick to go forward, and then he was dead this morning." She was clearly distraught and confused.

"You got off course a little, the settlement and mission is this way. We're going there and will take you." Elkanah motioned in a different direction.

Danica saw that the woman was lethargic and disheartened to the point of giving up. She said to Elkanah, "We have to let her rest a little, or she won't make it either."

"Here drink some of this." Danica offered the woman some water and then some strips of meat that Moses had roasted earlier. "

When the woman seemed stronger, they continued to head back to the mission. She was too weak to walk on her own and Danica and Elkanah walked with her to steady her. Her long dress was soggy, heavy and dirty from dragging it along the ground and from trudging through the forest. She was getting unusually weak so William stepped forward and carried her the last distance to the mission. She seemed grateful and realized they meant her no harm.

Danica and Elkanah were a short distance behind Moses, the woman and William, and out of earshot so Danica leaned in and whispered to Elkanah, "At least this bunch is nice."

He nodded, "We'll see."

When they arrived at the mission, Danica and Elkanah went in first while the survivors and the girls waited with William and Moses just inside the gates. Tah-Yah-Kee and his warriors lagged back just out of sight, still not wanting to unnerve the people even more.

They were surprised to see a noisy disturbance that appeared to surround the first group of survivors that were already at the mission. They were huddled together and talking in whispers.

Friar Simon was really disgusted by now and said to Elkanah, "You wouldn't believe what they have been up to just in the few hours since you left."

"Really?" Elkanah towered over the short friar and then leaned in closer to hear the news.

"Well, no sooner had you left and this one over there." The friar stopped speaking, turned and pointed across the room to the young widow, making it quite obvious that he meant her. "Well, she was literally caught with her skirts up, um-hum, yet again with the young Friar Tomas. They were being quite nasty if you ask me." He paused long enough to take another breath and turned to two others. "And those two over there were loudly arguing during our afternoon prayer. They were yelling and swearing over an item of little or no value, and it was just a horrible mess."

Danica silently listened, not wanting to miss one tidbit of Friar Simon's complaints. Danica felt like giggling when the young widow turned her way. She casually looked away as if she was not enjoying the conversation or listening, but not before noticing the woman's up tilted nose and dark, curly hair. Danica thought she was quite cute though, and wondered if the naïve young friar realized that this was probably her usual manner of behavior and most probably a habit. *Boy, is he going to be hurt if he finds that out,* Danica thought.

Elkanah shook his head. "Well, I hate to tell you this, but we are back so soon because we found more survivors down the beach."

The friar put his hand to his head, looked down and mumbled quietly and in disgust, "Please, not more of these people."

"I'm afraid so. Hopefully, this group will have more respect," Elkanah said.

The friar looked pale and was clearly tired of their unruliness. "Well, we shall see, but do bring them in. It's God's will that we offer charity to strangers in distress. I guess I can't blame these new ones for the way these here are behaving."

Elkanah nodded. "And we do have one here that needs immediate attention. We found her distraught after having to bury her dead husband. She's very frail and William ended up having to carry her."

"What happened to her husband?"

"He had severe stomach cramps and fever. He died during the night."

"Not good, but of course, bring her in so we can assist her."

By now, the newest survivors had already been taken into another large room where they were able to comfortably rest and wait for Friar Simon to assist them and show them to rooms with beds. Two other friars had already provided tea, boiled corn, peas, fish, bread and honey. Friar Simon let the other friars know of the woman's frail condition, and especially about the woman's husband that had died from the severe stomach cramps and fever. He thought it best that she be ministered to in separate quarters and away from the others because of the diseases that were beginning to spread among the people. Diseases were the last thing he wanted at the mission and knew it was best to take precautions.

The word was spreading about the new survivors and several friars gathered up some of the previous survivors and walked them over to the building where the weary new people were assembled together and waiting. Immediately, one young woman ran over to her sister and the two were hugging and crying. They both had given up hope of ever seeing each other again.

Another friar came in and brought in a few more people. Among them was a fairly young Duchess that hopefully searched for her cousin who was traveling with her but she just couldn't be found. She dismally excused herself and left the room. Also, one of the previous men eagerly greeted some of the new survivors and was happy to see that they had survived; but others were indifferent to him because they were only mildly acquainted before the ship wrecks. And then wouldn't you know – another friar came in with the widow in the black dress who threw herself crying, onto one of the skinny men.

"Oh, do look at this!" Friar Simon turned to Elkanah in disgust. "Just look at this." The friar motioned with his outstretched hand towards the couple; the sleeve of his habit brushed back and forth each time he moved his arm. "What a mess. The dead husband just came back from the grave."

Well, la dee dah, Danica thought. *This ought to be interesting.*

Elkanah frowned. "It is a mess.".

"Let me go and give this bad news to Friar Tomas right now." Friar Simon turned quickly and walked off with the bottom of his habit swinging out slightly behind him.

Dang, he's pissed. Danica was captivated by the drama and watched in fascination until he was out of sight.

Elkanah turned to Danica and said, "Friar Simon is clearly not going to tolerate this bad behavior."

"I see that." She shook her head in disbelief at all the confusion.

They didn't see Friar Tomas the rest of the evening but when Friar Simon returned, he said it didn't go well with Friar Tomas and he wishes to return to Spain with the woman.

Amazing, Danica thought.

They left the next morning early but not before having the friar send some men with a cart to the ship wrecks to salvage what they could for the survivors.

It didn't take long to get to the caverns. On the way, they passed some strange looking people that just stood staring at them as they passed by. Danica waved and shouted out a 'hello' to them but they didn't respond, but instead they snubbed them.

Tah-Yah-Kee just happened to be walking near Danica when this happened. He explained, "We call these the fish people because they have blue eyes like fish, and they changed my opinion about some white people because they are rude and smell bad."

"Ohhhhh, okay, if that's the way they want it." Danica rolled her eyes and was a little amused by that comment so she just looked the other way and made no more attempts to communicate with them.

They saw the lizard woman up ahead, near a cave, so they called out to her.

Danica was the first to speak. "Are you Nolia?"

The lizard woman tilted her head to the left as she slowly flicked her tongue and spoke in long drawn-out words. "Yes."

"Are you the gatekeeper to the lady from the stars?"

Nolia slowly tilted her head to the right. "Yes." She smacked between words.

Danica quickly assessed the situation. Nolia was human sized and she only slightly appeared to have lizard traits. Although she was mostly human, it was obvious that she had a little lizard dna and might be considered homely looking. However, Danica had mixed feelings about that and decided that *Nolia wasn't exactly ugly, but just slightly repulsive and slimy to look upon.* She held back a giggle realizing her own catty thoughts and promised herself to not do that again.

Danica moved in closer to Nolia and noticed her large, almond shaped, green eyes that were set into her narrow face. Oddly, her hairline was receding and did not grow at the temples and above her forehead. Her hairline started behind her ears and halfway up the back of her head. She had frizzy, short hair that had several bald patches, and her skin was definitely strange looking with brownish pink spots that matched her hair. *That's weird,* Danica thought stifling a giggle. She had a flat and wide nose that Danica had to force herself to 'not stare' at. And, the most peculiar thing of all was her perfect hour glass figure that most women would die for, big boobs and all. Danica suppressed a catty giggle again, *no tail though,* she thought and wished Jordan could see this. And strangely, Nolia had the slight appearance of having tiny scales that formed from the epidermis. She couldn't tell if it was actually scales, or just appeared that way. *Whatever,* Danica thought, trying to not laugh out loud and thought again, *Oh, my goodness, I wish Jordan could see this. She would love it.* She giggled for sure this time and looked at Elkanah to see if he had noticed. He didn't seem to.

Danica became so enthralled by the appearance of Nolia's funny looking mouth that she hardly noticed anything else after that. She had a top lip that was full in the front, and then skinny at the corners of her mouth. Her rich voice was throaty and she was slow speaking. She disgustingly smacked her lips between some of her words. Danica watched in fascination as Nolia rolled her head to the right when she spoke, and then back to the left as she spoke again, flicking her tongue. She said in an agonizingly slow way, "Go through the forest and past another stretch of beach, then through some woods with some tall pines. You will come to a clearing where you will find larger caverns. This is where you will find the lady from the stars." Nolia decided that it was okay to let Danica proceed.

"Thanks." They were eager to be on their way. After they were a good distance away, Danica asked Elkanah, "How did that happen to Nolia?"

"Who knows? There are a lot more just like her deep in the caverns, and Danica, stay away from her. She will kill you if she can."

"Really? Thanks for the warning. She seemed so nice."

"Well, she's not!" He straightened his spear and started walking. "Come on, let's go," he said and was way out ahead of them by the time Danica and the girls caught up with him.

The walking got tiresome, but Danica didn't complain because all she wanted to do was find the lady. Suddenly she was startled to see eyes peering through the trees at her. The sunlight was shining down through the trees and casting shadows. This made it hard to see the painted faces that blended in with the surroundings and they normally went undetected. It had almost worked, but one warrior blinked and moved just about the time Danica looked in his direction, and then they made eye contact. Moses saw that too and calmly said to Danica and the girls, "Act like you don't see them and keep walking. They're just curious."

They kept walking and finally came out of the forest and to the stretch of beach that Nolia had told them about. It was genuinely an exotic paradise. It had the whitest beaches and the most beautiful sand dunes she had ever seen. She couldn't resist the urge to take off her moccasins so she could wade along the edge of the water for a while. It felt so good to scrunch the beach sand beneath her feet and to feel the water sweep seaweed up and around her ankles. It did Danica's heart good to see that Irene and Charm were going barefooted and enjoying the sea breeze too. They laughed when seagulls swooped in around them, one made a nosedive and just missed them. The seagulls wanted any kind of handout and certainly made their presence known.

"Quick!" William was up ahead of them and motioned for them to go back towards the trees. Danica hurriedly put her moccasins back on and they ran past the sabal palms and into the woods but not before seeing the huge boat anchored with two smaller boats filled with men ready to swarm the beach.

They ran through the woods just along the edge of the trees trying to avoid any contact with these intruders. The girls tried to keep up but Danica was powerless to help them because one of the men came at her from out of nowhere. Before Danica had a chance to do anything, a rough looking man in ragged clothes had forced her to the ground and hurriedly bound her hands and feet together with a small rope.

"Run!" Danica yelled at the girls.

He took off after the two girls because he greedily wanted to sell the three of them. He knew the girls would bring good money because of their youth and fair hair. They would probably be bought to be used as servants or concubines.

He soon came back without the girls and it was not hard for Danica to realize that Elkanah and the others had the girls with them. When the ragged man reached for Danica, her hand shot out and sliced his face with the skinning knife that she had hidden in her moccasin. "Stupid, don't you know you're supposed to search a woman?" She pulled her knife back and plunged it into his throat, this time killing him. "And you should have tied my hands in the back stupid, not the front."

She saw Elkanah quickly push through the undergrowth, breaking twigs and branches with his club as he came through a thicket of briars. He moved through the shrubs and bushes as fast as he could towards her and gently grasped her arm and helped her to an upright position. He pulled her close to him and held her tight to his chest for a minute and then she felt his lips brush her cheek and hair. He said softly in her ear, "I thought he had killed you. The girls said he tied you up."

"He didn't search me. I had the skinning knife in my moccasin."

He held her even tighter for another moment and then let her go. She could feel her heart beating fast under her tunic, which was confusing to her.

He looked intently into her eyes and softly said, "You do amaze me," the troubled look was back in his eyes, "but hurry Danica, let's get out of here!"

Without hesitation, she grabbed her weapons and they ran until they finally caught up with the others.

CHAPTER 15

"Good grief, not you again!" Danica was truly disgusted and rolled her eyes. Assfeet was up ahead with some other trappers throwing dice, and gambling. They had their makeshift camp set up with furs loosely spread around. Even so, something smelled good roasting and they were all hungry. It turned out to be a large pig, and it was not that far from the beach so one of the others had a bucket of shrimp to roast on hot rocks. Assfeet took a shrimp out of the bucket and ate it raw. He was looking at Danica all the time. She took one look at him and hissed, "You better keep your stinking ass away from me. You totally gross me out."

She heard the laughter again. One of the trappers walked up to Danica and she noticed that he was dragging one foot. "He's harmless. He just ain't right in the head."

"Yeah right, and don't you come near me either."

Elkanah walked over to the trappers and in a firm voice said, "I'm serious, leave the girls alone. Don't go near them."

The trappers went back over to where they had been and left Danica and the girls alone for the rest of the evening.

The girls were hungry and gladly accepted the roast pig when Danica sliced them off a piece. They needed to keep building their strength back up if they were to make it back home.

Elkanah sat down with Danica and the girls to make sure the trappers didn't bother them again, and then the girls got some much-needed sleep. Actually, it was pretty quiet except for two of the trappers negotiating the trade of a beaver pelt for some much-wanted coffee.

Danica had that same dream again that night about Elkanah, except this time he was holding her in his arms and when his lips brushed against her cheek, her mouth hungrily turned to meet his. Her need for him was demanding, alive, and confusing.

They continued on their way the next morning, and eventually they came to a trail that would take them through the pines, and then to the caverns that housed the lady from the stars.

When they were approaching the caverns, a silly looking horned toad was darting back and forth across the path. Danica couldn't help but poke her foot at the horned thing and go "pssssst", thinking to scare it away, but it just stopped and stared at her. They went on around it and towards the caverns.

"And Danica, don't forget what I told you about Nolia and her kind? They live deep in the caverns, so don't wander off. Okay?" Elkanah said.

"Oh okay, I won't."

"And you might want to tell the girls to stay right here in the presence of William and Moses until we get back," he cautioned. "I've already told William and Moses to keep their eyes on the girls."

"I'll tell the girls right now."

After a few more minutes of discussion, Elkanah and Danica headed for the opening to the cave while their companions lingered just outside the entrance.

Right away, it struck them as odd to see some peculiar looking people coming and going; they were partially indifferent to each other as they were going in and out of the cave.

"What are these people doing?" she asked.

"Not sure."

Once they were inside the cave, they saw two fires that gave off some much-welcomed light. Their eyes had to adjust to the dim surroundings before they could move deeper into the cave and then into more darkness.

Loose stones shifted under their feet as they moved along with caution and deeper into the chilly, pitch-black unknown. Danica and Elkanah unsteadily felt their way along the cool and damp rock wall and dared to venture into an even more murky and dank area. There was an atrocious odor that Danica couldn't quite identify, and it was something she had never smelled before. The stench was particularly offensive as they came closer to the offending objects. It was some sort of garbage heap with unrecognizable things heaped on top of other putrefying things. It was enough to gag a maggot.

Without much warning, they rounded a curve in the tunnel and saw a faint light flickering inside a dismal and gloomy chamber. Once they entered this chamber, they noticed that some people were just standing around so Danica inquired of them to see if they knew where the lady from the stars might be. One man was standing beside the chamber entrance and seemed to be an odd sort. He pointed to the other side of the chamber and said, "You have to go under there." He continued to point towards a small opening that had severely rough edges. "Most people are afraid to go through there, but that's where she is."

"You mean under there?" Danica said with uncertainty and pointed towards the same opening that was not even three feet high and wide.

"Yes."

"How safe is it?" she said.

He shrugged and said, "Not very safe. You will see three winding tunnels once you get inside, and try to avoid the jagged rocks. I'm not sure which tunnel to take, but if you take the wrong one, it will lead to the lizards and you won't like that."

"Great, thanks for telling me,"she said with uncertainty. She turned towards the opening, and then as a second thought, she turned back to him and asked, "So, then you must know what happened to Nolia. How did she get that way?"

"Well, sorta. All I know is what I've heard. They all say that a kid wandered off into the caverns a long time ago. Nobody even knows for sure; it was so far back. But anyway, the kid – a girl – managed to survive by eating insects, snails and mice, you know." He spread both hands out as if to say 'go figure', and he rolled his eyes as if he didn't believe it himself. "However, there is a Nolia!" He spread his hands out again and then rolled his eyes again. "So, something unnatural did take place. They say she became friends with a little male lizard and somehow they managed to grow into adulthood together, and it's freakish to even think about the rest."

"You're so full of shit. You have no clue either." Danica rolled her eyes.

He laughed. "So you say."

"Well, how did Nolia get outside the caverns?"

"Not sure, there are more like Nolia. I just think some people brought them out just because they were curious. The ones that people brought out while they were young adapted to the light and weather outside. Anyway, once you go under there," he said, then paused and pointed again to the small opening. "You'll see an old geezer. Just ask him and he'll tell you where she is."

"Thanks." Then she mumbled under her breath, "I think."

When she turned back to Elkanah she thought there was a faint smile on his lips as if he was enjoying her conversation with this odd man, but he quickly regained his deadly serious demeanor.

"I don't know about this." She was shaking her head 'no' at the thoughts of going through the small opening with the jagged rocks.

"It's up to you. I can't fit under there," Elkanah said.

"I know."

They stood there for about fifteen minutes or so just deciding what to do next.

"I'm doing it!" she said handing her weaponry to Elkanah, everything but her knives.

She managed to slide under the small opening and then she crawled along on her belly through some cold pools of stagnant water until she finally saw a small light that lit up a small chamber. Inside the small chamber, she saw where someone had placed several torches, and inside the chamber were three tunnels, but she saw no old geezer.

She got to her feet and looked around. She quickly made her decision, took one of the torches, and then chose to follow the tunnel on the left. It was a bad choice. After Danica had gone several feet into the tunnel, she saw three lizard girls. They all had different human features, but they were still amazingly a lot like Nolia.

They were particularly impressive with their charming smiles and Danica felt herself choosing to let them draw her in to them, in spite of Elkanah's warnings. She felt herself trusting them. She accepted when they invited her into a larger chamber that was dazzling with stalagmites, which were mostly limestone rock formations that were rising from the floor of the cave. She had to duck to avoid stalactites hanging from the ceiling of the cave that were dripping water with calcium salts. In some spots, stalagmites were actually touching Stalactites.

The lizard girl that had the largest smile reached out and stroked her cheek and Danica couldn't help but think, *how sweet.*

One of the lizard girls offered Danica a pungent tasting drink that was a lot like lemonade, slightly sweetened, but much sourer than any lemon she had ever tasted. "We would like to talk to you, so please rest and be comfortable." She showed Danica a strange looking seat that was sunken in and almost looked like a hammock.

The beverage was hard to drink but Danica politely accepted it and sipped slowly on it anyway. She waited to see what they wanted to talk to her about.

The same lizard girl sweetly spoke again, "In the next chamber are our males that are eagerly awaiting our mating season and that time is almost here. I am officially assigned to choose the most perfect human female for them to mate with and reproduce our young. We want offspring with more human features and qualities, and I think you would be perfect. We prefer a human female that is muscular and not frail of mind. You see, the frail ones don't thrive here and usually die before they even give birth to their young."

Danica was stunned with horror. "Oh, hell no!" The thoughts of them wanting her to reproduce for them in this eternally dark place and with scant food sickened her. She jumped up to run but the lizard girls grabbed her and pulled her towards the opening of a foul-smelling area that was swarming with lively and repulsive lizards. The sweetest lizard girl twisted her arm until she screamed out in pain and they quickly overpowered her. She was surprised at the strength of these lizard girls and knew that if she went in there with the males, she would never come back out.

"I see that you are reluctant, so let's talk some more." They shoved her down into a chair near the opening that led to the male lizards. The lizard girls were moving about, not rushing her, and giving her time to get used to the idea because they thought she was so perfect for this. "This will be easier for you if you cooperate, because you see, our males like sweet, loving females to mate with. They don't like it if we have to use force."

"Well, I'm not sweet."

"You can work on it and try to be. Truly, it will be best for you."

Danica couldn't believe what was happening. She sat there in stunned silence and remembered that she had a small piece of aloe in her pocket. *I wonder,* she thought. Slowly and without drawing attention to what she was doing, she placed her hand in her pocket and squeezed the piece of aloe until she felt slick moisture on her fingers. She nonchalantly managed to rub some onto her arms without them paying much attention to what she was doing. When they grabbed at her this time, she was able to slide out of their grasp and run. Thanks to her experience in the trees with Rose Marie, she had become too fast for them. She ran for the opening and out the entrance to the other two tunnels.

Danica chose the tunnel on the right without lingering to put much thought into it. Right away, she heard the drip, drip of water falling into some more water, and the rock walls around her were wet with dripping water, but she continued in search of the lady of the stars. It was rather dark in this tunnel, but to her amazement, she could hear and barely make out the outlines of delightful children playing freely in a large pool of water that was in a wider area of the tunnel. They were splashing each other, and their squeals and giggles echoed off the walls. Danica stood in awe and wondered considerably about these children and then moved along to search for the lady of the stars.

The long tunnel curved and then she was right inside a spacious chamber that glittered with breathtaking reds, oranges, and black hues that melted into each other. Danica gasped at the beauty of the stalactite formations that hung from the ceiling of the cave and over to her right was a real old man that lit an even larger torch.

"Excuse me, sir. I'm looking for the lady of the stars. Can you help me?" Danica inquired of him supposing that he was the old geezer.

"Yes, she is right over there."

"Where, I don't see anything." She squinted trying to see what he was pointing at.

He held the torch out and towards the rocks near the side of the cave. "Look into the light."

"I don't see anything," she said.

He moved the light in closer to the rocks and said again, "Look into the light."

She moved in closer and looked directly into the light. About that time, Danica saw a slight movement or flutter from one of the rocks and then a transparent form started to open up. It had the appearance of angel wings or something. It was not angel wings though, but to the contrary, it was the 'something'. It was now becoming more visible, and clearly, this image was unfolding into a considerably strange, but comely female. Danica could now see more clearly. The lady of the stars had been balled up on the side of the wall, near the floor, and completely blended in with her surroundings. She just looked like any other part of the rock formations and was obscured by many small, as well as large, stalactites and stalagmites. Danica stared at the lady in disbelief as she continued to unball. She could now see that the wings were not wings at all, but her arms. They were long and slender. They unfolded with a pulsating rhythm and she understood that the lady of the stars could expand or contract at will. Danica's heart was racing as she realized that she had found her at last.

Danica watched in complete fascination as the lady of the stars slowly and elegantly continued to expand and rise up in height to about ten feet. Her face became more visible now, and was not quite so transparent, but her breathtaking dress was transparent and flowed like tentacles of glowing shades of orange, white, and peach with tinges of pink mixed together. Her bioluminescence was like a blanket that softly covered her entire being and Danica could clearly see that she had no hair, but her delicately formed and engaging face had small, but kind and soft eyes. Just below her flattering, linear nose was a perfectly situated mouth. It was delicate and looked just like an unopened rose bud.

She was looking right at Danica as if she could see right through her.

"I see and hear your thoughts and I hope you can hear my thoughts. Most humans can't hear at my higher level of vibrational frequency."

Danica's mouth felt parched and dry, and all she could do was nod.

"I know it might seem odd to you but this is how stars engage in communication. I sometimes go out at night to converse with other stars that have fallen to the earth, just as I did so long ago."

"You're really a star?" she incredulously said out loud.

"Yes."

"But I don't understand, this is so much to take in." Before Danica could even speak, the lady from the stars had answered her.

"I know, but I'll help you to understand. My name is Tresla, star of Carina Nebula from the Sagittarius-Carina arm of the Milky Way,

and I survived when my outermost layer exploded into a great supernova."

"But I don't understand. Who are you?" Danica was truly perplexed at this moment.

"Again, I am Tresla, the innermost core of my star. I survived inside the meteorite that landed here."

"What meteorite?"

"Right here, you are inside it."

"But, we're inside a cave?" Danica was in disbelief.

"Yes, true. However, when my meteorite crashed to earth, it crashed into the side of this cave. This tunnel you came through led you into my meteorite where my home is for now. As soon as all of my children have fully developed by unballing and gaining strength, we will return home."

"Stars are alive?"

"Yes, there is a seed of life created inside the core of every star when they are born. I do also understand that you are lost from your time and would like to go home, but before you make this decision, I would like for you to know more about me, because you do have a choice. Do you understand?"

"Not really."

Again, the lady of the stars answered before Danica could speak.

"There were others that came here before you and they chose to stay here, and I'll explain in a moment. But first, I want you to *understand that there is a little boy that came here through the same portal you came through, and he does want to go home; he just couldn't understand me like you understand me. He was frightened by my appearance and ran from me. He had escaped from the slave traders and then recaptured by them. Now, perhaps you can help him."*

"But how can I help him?" Danica said.

"I'll tell you where he is and then I'll let you decide how to rescue him. The slave traders have him tied up on the huge ship that is anchored in the bay. I have seen him at night when I go out to communicate with the other stars, and I have to be careful and not be seen by anyone that might harm me when I am outside my protective meteorite. I only go out at night now because the sailors would relentlessly chase me, and I was once captured in a sailor's net and he kept calling me 'mermaid'. It was created in me to be gentle and to not intentionally harm anything, but if I am touched, I have certain cells that release a self-protecting venom that is harmful. The sailor touched me, and in his anguish, I managed to get out of his net by constricting and going back into my protective ball. I succeeded in surviving against many heavy odds.

"I know you have a large number of questions for me but time is of the essence for the little boy. He is weak and will need to heal before making his journey back home. Quickly retrieve him and bring him to me, and then I will have you understand more about me."

"I'll try. But first, I'm curious. Why are all those kids out there in the tunnel playing in the pool of water?" Danica said.

"They are my children, and I am waiting for them to gain enough strength to return to our home. I am also waiting for my other developing babies to gain enough energy so they can unball and be able to endure the journey also."

Danica listened in stunned silence. "But how can that happen? I still don't understand."

"This meteorite is a remnant of my supernova explosion that collided with a molecular cloud, which is a stellar nursery, triggering shock waves that produced self-propagating star formations. When the explosion took place, it sent shocked matter traveling at high speeds; this is probably what caused some stellar embryo to attach and fuse with my meteorite. I have them swaddled in cells of gas and dust inside the meteorite walls. They have to remain undisturbed until they emerge one by one, and on their own, from their cells. From there, I place them in the pool of energized water that you saw in the tunnel. There they gain strength to make the journey back home. When you rescue the little boy, he can be placed in the pool of energized water with my children so he can gain his strength back."

"And this is a meteorite? Really?" Danica said.

"Yes, right here."

"Inside this cave?" Danica said out loud.

"Partially, my meteorite crashed into the side of this cave and broke into pieces that are scattered about. The portal that you came through is a portion of my meteorite that landed in the river where you slipped under the blue rainbow. The blue particles that you saw form into a blue rainbow was actually radiation of energy as a result of fast-moving subatomic particles."

Danica nodded in amazement.

"Now hurry. Get the boy and bring him into the cave and place him beside my children in the pool of water."

"I'll try." Danica made her way back out of the cave and found Elkanah and the others waiting for her there. They were all curious to know what had happened inside the cave.

"What happened?" Elkanah asked. "I was worried about you. It took so long. Are you okay?"

"Yes, I'm okay, but you're not going to believe this. Those bitches wanted me to mate with their male lizards. Look!" She held her arms out to show him the red marks on her arms.

"Look where they were squeezing my arms and wouldn't let me go," she said with disgust.

"What? How did you get away from them?" His eyes were wide in surprise.

"I ran. And wait until you hear about the lady from the stars."

"So then, you found her?"

"Yes, and there is a little boy that was stolen by the slave traders and they're in the huge boat docked in the bay. The lady said I need to rescue him and bring him back to the cave for strengthening. She says he is really weak at this point and wants to go back with me to my time and place in life."

"Really?" Elkanah intently listened.

"Oh, and get this, the lady actually has a name. It's Tresla, and she's elegant and tall. I'll fill you in later. Let's see if we can find this kid."

"We'll find him," Elkanah promised.

William spoke up, "I'll get Tah-Yah-Kee to have a few of his warriors scout ahead and see what they can find out, and in the meantime, I'll ask around and pretend to want to buy a slave."

"Sounds good to me," Elkanah said.

"I'll try to get them to bring him off the boat to sell him, and if so, we can probably get him that way," William said.

"Will they do that?" Danica asked.

"Yes, they have to bring him off the boat to sell him. Nobody would go on that boat willingly."

"Makes sense." Danica agreed.

CHAPTER 16

They walked for several miles and the sparkling white sand crunched under their feet while the seagulls actively searched for even a morsel of food to feast on. The cleansing breeze was like magical hands bathing her soul as they trekked on. They passed many sand dunes before they got a signal from one of Tah-Yah-Kee's warriors warning them of something up ahead.

William and Moses caught up with the other warriors and discussed possible solutions for rescuing the boy. Elkanah, Danica and the girls lingered back a short distance from them, making sure they would not be noticed together.

When they got sight of the boat, Danica was curious and moved on up closer to it, but just out of sight by staying back off the beach and near the woods. She saw it when they brought the boy out for William to inspect. They had the boy wrapped in ropes and he looked too thin and frail.

Danica remembered the scene from the river when she had killed the alligator. It was the day when she saw someone resembling a Spanish Conquistador wrap a rope around something or someone. Now it all made sense to her. She realized that she had witnessed it when they were tying the boy up. It had to have been just after the Conquistador turned pirate had kidnapped him, and then they were going to sell him to the slave traders. She had felt so spooked by it that she decided to not call out, and it was a good thing too, because she would have also become a slave to be traded off.

Elkanah came over to her to see what she was looking at.

"How convenient, they're bringing him off the boat." Danica pointed towards the eight men as they brought the boy out for William to inspect.

"Yes, it is convenient and we can easily overpower those men and get the boy. I will signal you and then you can grab him. There's no need to frighten him even more by having one of the warriors grab him. It'll work better if you get him."

Elkanah turned to Irene and Charm and said in a firm voice, "You two stay right here and don't move."

They both agreed.

It happened just that way. William distracted the slave traders and Tah-Yah-Kee and the others swooped in for the attack. Just that fast, Elkanah signaled to Danica so she could move in and get the boy.

"I'm here to help you, so don't be afraid." Danica cut his ropes and lifted him gently into her arms because he was so bone thin and pale. His blond hair fell in loose ringlets over her arm and was getting quite long. Danica could feel shivers coming from his little body as he hugged her tightly around her neck. She held him securely to her and ran as fast as she could. When she glanced back, she saw traders coming from the boat to see what the disturbance was about. Danica and the others were gone before the traders could even figure out what had happened.

Danica was still carrying the little boy when they returned to the cave, but before going inside, she found a good grassy spot to place the boy so he could rest and eat something. Moses brought the boy some water from the spring that so freely flowed from beside the cave. Many people were gathered around the spring so it was pretty easy for Moses to trade a pelt for provisions to give to the boy.

"I'm Danica and what's your name?" she gently asked the boy.

"Robby."

"And Robby, how did you get lost?"

"My dad and I went canoeing and our canoe turned over. And I don't know what happened. I was just here and some weird guys with helmets got me and tied me up. They took me a long way on their boat and then sold me to the other men." Robby looked down. "They were really mean to me."

"How long have you been here?" she asked.

"I don't know. A long time." He looked sad.

"Well Robby, I got lost too when my canoe turned over and I'm trying to figure out how to get back home."

"I want to go home too." He was near tears now.

"I know you do, and I'll do my best to get us both back home. See those two girls over there?" She pointed towards the girls they had taken from Chua's camp.

He nodded.

"That's Irene and Charm. They need to go home too. They were lost while canoeing, just like we were. So, let's try to get you stronger and then we'll all do our best to get home."

"Okay." He nodded again.

"Well, come on." Danica reached her hand out to Robby to help him up. "Let's go inside the cave. There is a pool of water in there that has other children playing in it. It's supposed to help you become stronger, and I want you to play too. Okay?"

"Okay.

Danica picked Robby up and went inside the cave. She remembered exactly which tunnel to take to get back to where the children were playing. Without a word, she put the little boy into the water with Tresla's children so the strengthening could begin. She sat down on the edge of a large rock that was jutting out from some other larger rocks and watched Robby for a while. It was no time at all and Robby was giggling and playing with the other children.

"I'll be back in a little while. I'm just going into the next chamber." Robby was too busy playing with the other children to notice when she slipped away to see Tresla.

"I have the boy." Danica eagerly approached Tresla.

"Yes, I know. I was waiting for your return."

Just about that time a small movement from the side of the wall caught Danica's attention. Little tiny bumps were balled up all along each wall and one was just beginning to unfold. It looked like part of the rocks and it was unfolding just like Tresla had done. Small amounts of wavering light was beginning to shine faintly through a crack in a rock and it revealed a tiny transparent being that began to open up.

"What the heck," Danica whispered.

"This is one of my babies being born. These all along the walls are my other sleeping babies. They were able to survive the crash by being balled up inside their outermost part that was filled with stellar gas and dust. Somehow, they had attached to my outermost parts when I exploded. I was able to rescue them and place them here inside this highly protective chamber that is part of my meteorite. When I crashed into this cave, my meteorite and the cave merged to form a single entity. So now, when they are strong enough, they will emerge from their protective balls and then I will place them with the other children in the pool of energized water to complete their growth. Are you beginning to understand now?"

"Yes."

"Look over here Danica." Tresla's arm moved in a wavy motion when she turned to point out something.

Danica saw rows and rows of small cells on the wall that oddly looked like parts of the rock behind Tresla. Danica couldn't speak; it was all she could do to take this in and understand it.

"Come in with me and I will help you to understand more."

Tresla moved over closer to a small cell in the very center of the wall. It was just a small opening, just large enough for Danica to squeeze through. On this same wall were many other cells that resembled a honeycomb with hexagonal prismatic cells. Tresla went into the cell first by constricting her body. Danica followed and immediately sucked in her breath in astonishment at the vastness and majesty that opened up before her as she realized that space and size meant nothing inside the cells and their bodies were proportional to the space inside the cell. It was obviously Tresla's abode. Danica took several steps forward and was without a doubt inside a large palace.

"The other cells you saw belong to my children once they have matured enough to leave the pool of energized water. They will then be assigned to their own personal cell to wait for the other children to become strong enough to join us as we travel back to our home in the Sagittarius-Carina arm of the Milky Way.

"I know this is a lot to take in, and I know you want to know how to get home to your place and time, but before you can do that, you need to find out what brought you through to this time and place. This knowledge is the only thing that can free you."

"I don't know what caused it." Danica was truly puzzled.

"Think about it, and in the meantime, I will show you the springs that my children swim in after they leave the smaller pool of water."

Tresla showed Danica a doorway that led into more tunnels, and eventually they reached a huge opening that led out into a paradise with luscious green plants and flowers. And then oddly, into a small but picturesque hamlet. In the middle of this hamlet was a large spring with an astonishing waterfall.

To Danica's amazement, there were men, women, and children of all races that were vacationing there. Some were frolicking under the waterfall that splashed into an effervescent pool of water. Some were wading barefoot, and splashing water about, and washing in the nearby springs of water that was coming from the rock. Danica couldn't resist the urge to fill her water bottle from the water that was flowing from the rock.

Danica was absolutely staggered by all of this. Everyone was completely in one accord and with no hostility among themselves.

"What is this?" Danica breathed out in disbelief.

"These people are being energized in my children's springs of water. When my children leave the baby pool, they come here for a while. And then when they have developed even more, I take them for swims in the underground springs that flow for miles and miles under the grounds and caverns. They flow in all directions."

"Unbelievable!"

Tresla already knew the questions forming in Danica's mind, so she answered graciously. *"You're wondering why the others are here swimming and I'll tell you why. My energy has energized these pools of water so my children can survive and fully develop. Over time, all types of people would come here for water and noticed that if they had pain in their bodies, it would leave them while bathing here. My energy revitalizes them. The word soon spread about the rejuvenating waters here at this spring, and they started calling it 'the fountain of youth' which is really part of my children's developmental process and anyone that swims with my children benefits from it and feels youthful again. They are made welcome to stay and take advantage of this. However, when I leave here with my babies, the energy will start to subside gradually over time and eventually be gone entirely.*

"Danica, I also know the thoughts you have about the predicament you are in, and how you came to be here today. I do intend to help you.

"I want you to understand that when you were still there in your time I had already left here with my babies and gone back to take my place among the other stars. I was waiting until my babies had developed enough to make the journey safely back home. I did not want even one lost during the journey.

"You are wondering how this can be when it takes millions of years for a meteorite to eventually make its way to earth. Well, I'll help you to understand this. Time does not mean the same thing to

me as it does to you. Now that I am free from the meteorite, it is simple for me to travel at speeds that are unthinkable to you, but to me it is all possible.

"I'll help you to also see that during your time, there is very little of my energy left in the springs and river surrounding the rock that you slipped under when you came through to this time and place. That little fraction of energy that is still left in your time, along with some item you may have in your possession added enough energy to bring you through. That item also determined the time and place where you slipped through the weak-tear in space-time. Now, we need to determine what that item is."

"Wow!" Is all Danica could say.

"What did you have on you when you came through to this time?"

"Just the usual, my cell phone, water, compass, just stuff like that."

"Nothing else?"

Danica remembered the little bird pendant and arrows she had picked up that day while metal detecting and reached into her pocket to see if they were still there. To her relief they were still there. She took them out of her pocket and held them out for Tresla to see. "I found these the day I fell into the water."

"Danica, I understand now. This is only half of a pendant and has strong beliefs surrounding it. It has a mate. Now, all you have to do

is find the person that has the other half of this pendant and when you do, you will find the other half of your heart."

"What! This is incredible!" Danica said in disbelief and then settled into a stunned silence.

"And Danica, when you find the other half, and its owner, you will need for him to release you so you can leave this place and time. You will question this, but it was his great longing that brought you through. He wants the other half of his heart. It was his intense energy, blended with the energy from the meteorite, that brought you through the tear in space-time and to this time and place. He will have to release you, and then, if you choose to come back, it will be your free choice."

"Wow," was all Danica could say.

"When you find him, and if he releases you, you will then go back to the river where you came through before, and go back home the very same way you came here. You will need to have the pendant in your possession–it's that simple. Hold tight to the children and they can go back with you."

"I'm just so shocked I don't know what to say."

"I know, and Danica, one more thing before you start your journey back home. I want you to know-that I know-the times you would look up into the night sky and wish upon a star. I know this because I am your star. That's why you can communicate with me. And, I want you to know that when you would turn your smiling face

212

towards the sky and smile at me, I was always smiling back at you. Goodbye Danica, you will find your way back home, but most importantly, follow your heart."

"Goodbye Tresla, and thank you." Danica's heart was overflowing with gratitude. She smiled all the way out of the cave and found the others patiently waiting for her.

She saw Elkanah's questioning face first. "What happened?" Elkanah saw that her face was very pale.

She went straight to him. "It was awesome and freakish all at the same time. I just don't have the words to tell it all. You won't believe it! I still don't believe it."

"What? Tell me, did she tell you how to return?"

"Yes, but I have to find someone that has the other half of a pendant I have."

"Where is the pendant?"

"Right here, in my pocket." But the others crowded around her before she had a chance to unzip her pocket to show Elkanah.

Irene was the first to speak, "Did you find the lady? Can we get back home?" They were all trying to ask questions at the same time and it was impossible for Danica to answer them all.

"Yes, I did find the lady and we can probably make it back home."

"Probably?" Irene frowned.

"I have to work on it, but right now I have to find a place to rest. I'm just tired, but it did go well with the lady." Danica smiled. "She's a star and her name is Tresla, but she said everyone calls her the lady from the stars."

They gave each other puzzled looks, but Danica was still pondering her visit with Tresla and she kept most of the conversation private and in her heart and thoughts only. She was still just too stunned by it all.

All she wanted to do now was just sit down somewhere and rest. She made her way over to the grassy area where Irene, Charm and Robby had rested earlier, and as exhausted as she was, she didn't even care if questions were still coming at her. She just wanted to sleep, so she pulled her fur from her pouch. The scent of Elkanah was still on the soft fur, and a safe sleep came quickly. Danica never even woke up throughout the entire night, not until one of the girls nudged her awake.

Elkanah was close by, and they discussed the physical condition of the girls and boy. They were trying to determine if they would be able to make it back to the settlement where Jonathan and Fleur lived. They discussed at length the dangers they would face, but at least they didn't have to deal with Chua and his warriors anymore. They also knew where the pirates and the slave traders had their boats docked so it would not be difficult to avoid them. It would just be slower going back with Irene, Charm, and Robby. However, they would be able to rest for a while at the missions and at Queen Sushaney's village.

CHAPTER 17

They headed back towards the mission pretty early that morning and Elkanah walked ahead with William and Moses. Danica stayed close to the girls and boy, and all went well after they managed to get past Nolia. She was pissed because Danica refused to produce the spawn of lizards for them. Nolia clearly would have killed her if she could.

They walked for about two hours without stopping, that is, until they saw her.

"Look at that! It's Nolia and her lizard friends." Elkanah jumped up to get a better look.

They had been resting near a grassy field along with the others they were escorting to the mission.

"Oh no, not the bitches again." Danica just shook her head.

Elkanah nodded and motioned for Danica and the others to get back and stay down.

"She smells you."

"What the heck!" Danica looked puzzled.

Elkanah nodded. He put a comforting arm around Danica and pulled her close to him. She felt weak at his touch

"I'm not going to let anything happen to you. Let's go this way," he said moving her and the others in the opposite direction from Nolia and the bitches.

"Will they follow us?"

"No, they won't get too far from the cave."

"Good."

They eventually got back onto their path going towards the mission when a Panther almost attacked the boy. Danica had noticed the cat earlier when it had silently crossed the trail up ahead of them and that put her on alert. She knew the nature of this particular cat and its sneakiness. She also knew what it was capable of doing and it would be sudden. She drew her club and had it ready, but not too soon. Instantaneously, the cat made its appearance through some thickets and there was no doubt that his prey was the boy. The cat ravenously eyed him. It made a careful step forward and that was Danica's cue to aim her club towards the cat's head. She raised the club back behind her head with both hands and without hesitating, she threw it. The club made two spins before impact and crimson blood spattered from the cat's head.

Irene's and Charm's terrified screams brought Elkanah running back to see what was happening, and just that quick Danica was skillfully skinning the cat for the fur and to roast the meat over a fire.

After the much-needed rest and food, they set out again on their journey back. Backtracking didn't seem to be that bad to Danica because she now knew what to expect and where they were going. She looked forward to a bath at the stream they would reach soon.

She did have to carry the boy a lot, and then Elkanah took over and carried him part of the way. Moses offered to carry him too, and eventually, they came back to the stream where they rested and bathed before proceeding to cross over it.

Luckily for Danica, Elkanah was behind her when she slipped on the slippery rocks. "Hold on. I've got you." His arms went around her and held her tight to him to steady her, and then he seemed to just linger there holding her – she felt his breath on her hair and she strangely wanted the moment to not end. She thought that he was making sure she had a steady footing before he let her go, and maybe he was, but his arms seemed to tell a different story. They promised so much more if she would dare to let herself go there. She felt the strangeness of this man's body against her body, and the heartbeat of this man that so proudly wore feathers and silver jewelry in this wilderness. She felt the secret promises that his body made to her body. A secret desire made its way into her heart, never to leave her again. She wrestled with her own emotions as she became locked forever in that moment, in his arms, when his face and lips rested on her hair and cheek. After what seemed like forever, and after he saw that she was able to stand again on her own, he loosened his hold on her and stepped back a little from her. "Okay?"

She nodded. Her heart was racing and not only from fear of him this time.

The next day it was getting tiresome for the girls but Danica knew they were not that far now from a nice stretch of beach that would be refreshing, and then shortly after that, they would reach the mission where the friars could help them with the children.

The weary travelers finally reached the mission and were a little surprised to see that the ship wreck survivors were still there. "Humm, still here," Danica said as they walked past the chapel and then past the courtyard where several of the women were resting and enjoying the sun. They recognized one of the women as the last survivor they had found on the trail earlier; the one that was burying her husband. She still looked unusually thin.

As they came closer, the woman waved to them and they walked over to inquire about her well being. After a few minutes they moved along and William lingered there a moment longer than the others.

"Let's find the friar and see how this has been going," Elkanah said.

They walked on past the storehouse where they kept grains and other provisions, then past a large building that had the smell of fresh corn boiling and beside that were several beehive ovens with pumpkin bread baking.

About that time Friar Simon saw them approaching. He could barely contain himself and ran out to meet them. He blurted out the most recent news, "After you left here, there has been such a commotion around here that you wouldn't believe. These ship wreck survivors are so disorderly and disruptive." He threw up his hands. "They just won't leave each other alone. It's just unbelievable! And, now I have received word that the ship I had hoped they would leave on never made it here to rescue these people. It is presumed that the ship has met with misfortune I can't even let myself think about that because it would be too depressing if that were the case. It is predicted that it could take up to 3 years for another rescue ship to reach us. I don't know what we're going to do with these people."

"Why? What happened?" Elkanah asked.

"Well, I don't know about the ship, but you know the trunk that was salvaged? The one that said Sophia?"

Elkanah nodded.

"Uh-huh, well, it clearly belongs to Duchess Sophia and don't you know that somebody has already stolen her jewelry and most of her clothes. It's disgraceful. Just disgraceful. And now, Friar Tomas is saying he is in love with this widow that turned out to not be a widow. He says he doesn't care that she has a husband."

The friar paused and leaned in closer to Elkanah, "And now rumor has it that she is with child."

"What?"

"Uh-huh. Yes, what a mess. Uh-huh, and now her husband is upset and wanting to fight Friar Tomas. Can you believe this? Fight with a friar? Ungodly to say the least. I have to get these people out of here."

Another friar walked over and whispered something into Friar Simon's ear. Friar Simon nodded and handed the prayer book he had been holding over to the other friar.

After the friar walked away, Friar Simon continued, "Let's talk more after mass."

"Sure."

Much later that evening, Friar Simon continued the conversation. "I just don't see how we can keep Friar Tomas here any longer. His lack of wisdom is causing much unrest. Would you escort him to the other mission with a letter to Friar James when you go? Perhaps from there he will come to his senses and comprehend the wrong he is doing. Anyway, from there he can await a different ship to return to Spain and away from this situation. And also, the letter is to let Friar James know about the Duchess. She is to marry a Captain Lundquist at the settlement that is near his mission and he should be quite happy to hear that she is here and safe. He will be happy to make arrangements to come get her."

"Of course, and yes, I think it would be a good idea for Friar Tomas to be removed from this situation. Does he know yet what you suggest?" Elkanah asked.

"No, and he won't like it, but maybe with some contemplative prayer he will come to realize what God will have him to do."

"I see. I'm sure you're right. We will escort him there." Elkanah said.

"Good. And also, the other friars and I have discussed this at length and we have determined that these other survivors should be relocated to other and more thriving colonies in other areas. From there they can wait for a ship or learn to thrive there." His facial expression showed his displeasure at the whole situation and he made a motion with his hand as if to say 'this is all absurd'. "What are your thoughts on this, and will you help us?"

"I think you are right. We should be able to find places for them. I'll let William and Moses know about it." Elkanah said.

"Okay."

"And if Friar Tomas doesn't want to go?" Elkanah asked.

"He should go. It's best for everyone involved," the friar said.

"I agree."

"I'll go and speak with him and make sure he is ready to go when you are." Friar Simon seemed happy about this decision.

The next morning several friars had gathered with Friar Simon in the courtyard and was in serious discussion about Friar Tomas. Finally, and reluctantly, Friar Tomas came outside.

Friar Simon motioned for Friar Tomas to come over. "We are serious about what we discussed with you last night. You will have to leave here because of the trouble caused by you and the woman, but you already know the seriousness of this. And what you do after you leave here is up to you. I strongly encourage you to seriously pray about this. However, after you get back to Spain, you and the woman can then decide what you will do, but I assure you, she has already said she wishes to remain with her husband."

Friar Tomas said, "But I want to stay here with her; she said she wants to be with me."

"I know you do, but you can't do that."

He did not want to go and resisted, but only for a moment. Moses and William walked over to him and Moses spoke, "Friar Simon wants you to go with us to the other mission. We are leaving now."

Elkanah walked over. "Is everybody ready to go?"

Friar Tomas went along with them but with a lack of enthusiasm. Each step he took appeared to be agonizingly painful for him to leave the mission and the woman. He was especially remorseful because he didn't get to talk to her before leaving. He knew that turning back was not an option and he knew that he was no longer welcome there. Nor was the woman.

"He looks very sad," Danica said to Elkanah.

"He is, but he knew better. He knew that if found out, the other friars would not condone that sort of conduct. They say it is offensively immoral and a stumbling block before others for a friar to behave in this fashion."

"Yes, I see that," she said.

After they were outside the mission, they walked for about two hours, and because Chua and his men were no longer a threat, they were able to take a short cut down through some woods and towards a short beach. The path they walked eventually intersected with another path where they saw about thirty young and demure appearing women walking towards the beach. Danica and the rest waited until all the women had crossed the path in front of them. The women cautiously walked down a narrow path that led through large clumps of sandspurs, and then through scattered sea oats, and then finally into the edge of the water. Noisy seagulls swooped in close to the women in hopes of getting a bite of anything, especially the snails, scallops and oysters that they were gathering for that night's celebration.

The young women didn't even look at Danica and Elkanah, but kept walking as if they didn't dare look aside from their job of picking up the shell fish.

"They didn't even look at us," Danica said.

"They are just wary of strangers and don't want to become the pirate's concubines. They never know what to expect."

"So, then I have another question. You know, I'm just curious."

"Okay."

"Why are we all so well received by the friars? It's just confusing. There is so much fighting and all. It seems like everybody is trying to kill everybody else. Why is that?"

"First, let me answer this. We are well received by the friars because they are converting natives to Catholicism. It's complex, and they are on friendly terms with my mother and people. My mother has on several occasions provided the missions with corn and peas when their provisions were running low. Some friars were actually starving while waiting for their ships to come in carrying provisions. But that was quite a while back. Everything is okay at the moment. Especially with Chua gone from this world; it will be better."

"But isn't this dangerous for the friars?"

"Yes, extremely so. Some have been killed by natives that refused to be converted and give up their own customs and ways of doing things."

"Yikes."

"Yes, brutal deaths."

The next day it was getting tiresome for the girls but Danica knew that they were not that far now from Tah-Yah-Kee's camp where fresh horses would be waiting. It was also fortunate for them because there was not even one dust worm out feeding in the wide-open field just before coming into the camp.

Danica knew the girls didn't have the strength to run across the field and she wondered how they would make it. About that time, she saw Moses, along with two tall and muscular warriors come over to the girls. Moses spoke to the girls for a moment and then one of the warriors picked Charm up and ran with her across the field. Just as quickly, the other warrior picked Irene up and ran with her. That sight was reassuring to Danica because she knew the girls would not have made it on their own. Elkanah ran with the boy, two other warriors assisted the friar because of his habit that could have easily become tangled up in briars and weeds. However, it was all done without problems.

Several of Tah-Yah-Kee's scouts had gone ahead to make sure some of the women were waiting to assist the girls and boy by making them comfortable with much needed food and drink. They still needed to regain their strength so they could endure the anticipated journey back to Jonathan's and Fleur's settlement.

The girls badly needed the rest because they were still weak physically and mentally from Chua and his warrior's constant threats of abuse and the rapes which came all too often. Danica had noticed when they went back through the mission how frail they still were.

And then later they had to crawl down some rough terrain and one of the girls hurt her ankle. The boy on the other hand, seemed to be getting into better spirits and was actually feeling stronger and a little adventuresome. He was getting some nice pink color back into his pale skin.

Anyway, after a substantial rest at Tah-Yah-Kee's village, they set out on horseback. The two girls were on the same horse and Elkanah led them along after he realized they had never been on a horse alone before. Danica had the boy with her on Arrow, Queen Sushaney's horse.

They came to a large open field beside some trees, and just over to the right, and much to Danica's disgust, she saw pelts stretched out on limbs. And then she saw him. "Oh gross, not you again!"

"Don't even look at him," Danica said to the girls.

Assfeet giggled like a little girl when they passed by him and they looked the other way without looking at him. He was just standing there taking a whiz right in front of them. By now, Danica was coming to realize that he was not a threat, just stupid. *Or,* she thought, *not right in the head or stupid? Which is it? Yep, just stupid.*

"You're so disgusting. Just stay away from us." Danica rolled her eyes.

Elkanah did stop and have some words with Assfeet and then he came back to Danica. "Hold up. He just wants to know if we have furs to trade. Do you want to trade your Panther fur?"

She stopped her horse. "For what?"

"He has coffee."

"Okay, that's a no brainer. Let's do it." She handed the fur to Elkanah so he could make the trade.

CHAPTER 18

It was a relief to them all when they reached Queen Sushaney's village where they all received a great welcome. Tah-Yah-Kee's warriors mingled in with the hundreds of other warriors that were busy doing different things, and Danica didn't even notice when William and Moses eased away to join the others.

However, a little earlier, William had made his intentions clear. "I'll be going back to the mission," he said.

"Because of the woman that buried her husband?" Elkanah asked.

"Yes, she asked me to not leave her. I told her I had to stay with everyone." He motioned towards Elkanah, Danica and Moses. "And besides that, she was too weak to go forward."

"She's afraid." Danica knew full well what that was like.

"Yes, she is," William said, "and I think she will have better chances of survival in Virginia. I think I'll take her there. My uncle is there with his wife and children and I'm sure they will welcome her into that colony."

"Sounds good." Elkanah said, they all agreed.

Up ahead, Danica saw Queen Sushaney standing at the entrance of her hut waiting for her son's arrival. Elkanah, Danica, Tah-Yah-Kee, the friar, Irene, Charm, and Robby were quickly escorted into the queen's large hut where several women had large baskets of fruit, vegetables, dried venison and alligator. The alligator was the top choice and delicious.

"Rest here," Queen Sushaney said graciously to Danica and motioned around the room towards mats that they could rest on after the large meal.

She turned to Elkanah and Tah-Yah-Kee and motioned towards another room of the huge hut. "Let's discuss Chua and my trophies you have for me." Queen Sushaney led them into the other room and out of earshot of the friar, and the girls and boy. Danica was not too thrilled at the thoughts of seeing the trophies again–Chua's eyes and earrings. She chose to stay with the others for some much-needed rest.

That evening, Elkanah took Danica along with the boy and girls to the same hut at the back of the camp that Danica had stayed in before. The friar had his own hut. There were several warriors posted nearby to guard them and to keep them safe. After the boy and girls were asleep, Danica couldn't resist the urge to join the festivities later that night.

Fires were flickering in a soothing way that seemed to suggest that all was peaceful and well throughout the camp, but by now Danica knew for sure that the possibility of war was causing every warrior to be in an agitated state of suspense and alert. Danica could feel this tense undercurrent of hostility now, as never before and noticed suspicious whispers. She heard the word Danuwa a lot, suggesting that more wars were coming. She had learned from Elkanah how to recognize certain gestures and tones of voices and to be watchful for possible danger. Even so, with all of the agitation surrounding her, she still enjoyed the ceremonies and she especially enjoyed dancing around the fires.

Danica heard a soft laugh and turned to see Elkanah standing there with amusement in his eyes. She realized that this was the first time she had heard him laugh and she also noticed that he was wearing a new headdress with different and more colorful feathers. The fabric was still red and white but had some yellow threads woven throughout it.

"Danica, it's good to see you have some fun."

She smiled. "I haven't had fun in a long time. I like this."

They both sat down on log benches that were in a circle around the area where the ceremonies took place. Some were rough with uneven and irregular surfaces, but they were still impressive and were throughout the entire village. And then there were others that were artistically decorated with different designs that were painted with vibrant blues, yellows, greens, and reds.

They silently watched the festivities for a while and at the same time, she silently watched him. She sensed, rather than actually saw, how the most minute details and sounds didn't go unnoticed by him. The fingers of his left hand gently brushed at a loose strand of his black hair and then his fingers slowly moved across his forehead barely touching his skin. Her eyes moved over his face and then rested on his full lips. She had the shocking thought that she would like to taste those lips, and then she remembered her dreams and felt a warmth go through her entire body. Almost embarrassed again, she quickly brushed those thoughts aside.

Elkanah broke their silence, "So, this is what we do for fun. What did you do for fun where you came from?"

"Oh, I used to go canoeing a lot with my cousin and shooting at the range with my grandparents."

"Shooting what? What is at the range?" He leaned in closer intently listening to every word.

"We would shoot guns and the bow and arrows. The range is a place indoors where we would go to practice shooting our weapons."

"Oh, I see, so then, all of the women where you come from use bows and guns?"

"Oh no, not at all. I just happened to have grandparents that taught me how?"

"Really, why?"

"Because my grandparents were in the Navy and my grandpa was a Navy SEAL. The Navy is a branch of the military. My grandmother got out of the Navy early and my grandfather stayed in longer. So, I grew up with guns around, but no, not all women and not even all men shoot guns where I come from. Do you know what the Navy is?"

"Yes, I've heard my father speak of Navy ships of England, but what are SEALs?

"SEALs have special training to operate in difficult situations, primarily the sea, air, and land. In other words, my grandpa was a great swimmer."

"Oh, okay. So, how about your parents?"

"My mother died when I was young and I never knew my father."

"Too bad, I'm sorry about that." He seemed to genuinely care.

"Anyway, I meant to ask you before, but getting everyone back here safely was the main issue. So, what did Tresla say? How do you get back home?"

"I'm not sure. She said I have to go back to the same exact spot where I came through and I have to have the same object that brought me through," Danica said.

"And what is that object?" Elkanah asked and spread his hands out in a questioning way. Danica couldn't help but admire his eloquent speech that was a lot like Jonathan's, and she assumed that it was a lot like their father's.

"I don't know. Maybe a little pendant I found the day my canoe turned over. I also found arrow heads in the sand by the river," she said.

"Really? And what did she say about it?" A puzzled look was in his eyes.

"That there is a mate to it, and that mate is the other half of my heart. My guess is that it's just another superstition."

"Really? And what else did she say?"

"I don't know. She said so much it would be hard to repeat. Anyway, it's getting cold, so I think I'll turn in." Danica shivered.

"Let me walk you over to your hut," he said.

"Sure. I guess we have a long day ahead of us tomorrow," she said.

They both headed back towards her hut and it was pretty quiet as they got closer to the back of the village and away from the fires and festivities.

Elkanah stopped walking and turned to Danica; he had that serious and troubled look again. "Danica, do you remember the day you slipped on the rocks at the stream?"

"Yes." She had turned to look at him now waiting to see what he was going to say.

"Maybe I shouldn't say this, but I wanted to kiss you that day." She saw his seriousness and turned to walk away because she didn't trust her own emotional well-being after Alex.

He lightly touched her arm and turned her to face him and said, "Please don't walk away Danica. Let's talk. I don't want you to be afraid of me." He touched her hand and she felt the warmth of his fingers against her skin. His large hand was now covering hers and he said, "Tell me Danica, that you're not afraid of me anymore."

"I'm not," she said while shaking her head no. She was trembling now and knew that this was the truth, but now she was more terrified of her own emotions.

"Good."

He intently looked into her eyes to see if he could even see one spark of feelings. He gradually pulled her closer to him and with his right hand he brushed the hair back from her face. She felt the warmth again from his palm; this time against her neck. "Danica, you know I'm falling in love with you and I fear it won't be returned."

Every moment was in slow motion now as he gently lifted her up so she was standing on one of the lower benches and he pulled her body closer to his. She couldn't speak; all she was aware of was the way his body felt touching her body. Weakness was closing in as his face came closer and closer to her face. The musky smell of soft leather was pleasant to her senses and his arms felt safe around her.

Her heart raced as a burning sensation shot throughout her entire body. It happened just like it did in her dreams; his lips brushed her cheek and lips, and then his lips touched her lips again and lingered there. He kissed her in a way that left no doubt about his feelings for her. She couldn't hold her emotions back any longer. She kissed him back in a way that told him she wanted more of his embraces.

She didn't resist when he led her into his hut and tenderly kissed her again; she melted into his arms. Her responsive kisses said what words couldn't say and by now he was kissing her with a fierce and demanding passion. He took her that night and this too was just like in her dreams. He was above her and his long hair had come loose and gently slid down her cheeks covering her face as they made love. This touch set off something that was untamed and bold, something that was animal like and hungry. Early the next morning Elkanah set off that same flood of strange emotions in Danica again, and she wondered how, and if she could ever leave him now.

CHAPTER 19

They left around midmorning and her heart ached at the thoughts of leaving him and this land to go back home, but she had no choice. The boy and girls had to go back, and her heart was torn apart thinking about her grandpa, Josh, Jordan and now Elkanah. She loved them all.

Because of the girls and boy, they made the decision to take the longer path back and go around the area that was the habitat for the dangerous Lynxes. It was a good choice because they enjoyed the beauty of the longer and much more used path.

They crossed the river by raft and saw many colorful and musical parrots flying about and some were in the trees and any place they could settle or congregate to rest for a while. As Danica and the others approached the birds, the squawking became increasingly loud. Some were making gurgling sounds; others made sharp screeches, while others were happily singing. The yellows, oranges, and reds on their heads and bodies were astonishing in quality and their blue and green tail feathers were completely stunning.

Danica and the others just lingered there enjoying the splendor of the views. In addition to this breathtaking event, the grassy, small rolling hills looked so inviting that they decided to rest there for a while and enjoy a refreshing bath in a lake. It was such a welcomed sunny day so they washed some articles of clothing and hung them to dry on lower tree branches.

The friar found a spot a little distance from the others where he could bathe in private. Danica noticed that he actually took his sandals off and waded in the shallow water. She did feel a little sorry for him, but realized that he had a serious decision to make with his own life and future. She hoped he would make the right decision. *Oh well,* she thought, *not my decision.*

After the desired baths, they made a fire to roast the deer Elkanah had speared at the edge of the woods. It was larger than any deer Danica had ever seen, and its distinctive flavor was pleasantly tasty along with some cabbage palm she had managed to reach along the way. They had needed that revitalizing rest and from there they made it to the mission without any problems, except the panther. It was not exactly a problem yet, but when Danica saw it, she went ahead and killed it because she knew it was too unpredictable. It was huge, and the fur was sleek and beautiful.

When they arrived at the mission, the girls giggled when they saw a couple of the hostile braves moon the friar. Apparently, this striking performance was a common happening and Danica couldn't resist the urge to laugh along with them. As it turned out, it was amusing even to the friar because it had happened so often these days.

"Wait here," Elkanah said to the others.

He immediately went to find Friar James and handed him the letter. "I think you need to see this. It's from Friar Simon. They were experiencing an awkward situation at the other mission. Most unusual."

The friar carefully read the letter. Elkanah could see the shock in his face.

"Where is the young friar in question?"

"Waiting with the others."

"Also, it says here that a Duchess Sophia was rescued from the ship wreck and has come here to marry Captain Lundquist," the friar continued.

"Yes, she was there at the mission and is eager to leave there."

"I'll get word to him so he can arrange to get her here. This will make him happy." He smiled, "I wonder how well the Duchess knew Captain Lundquist before consenting to marry him?"

"I don't know. Friar Simon didn't say. He was just eager for them all to leave. However, Duchess Sophia didn't seem to be a problem. Why?" Elkanah said.

"Well, it's because Captain Lundquist is a talkative person and thinks he knows everything. He is calculating, avaricious and wants to control everything. However, he is extremely pleasant and respectful of the women so as not to offend them. So, I guess all will be well."

"Good. Well, let's go out and get Friar Tomas for you," Elkanah said.

"Yes, hopefully the friars here can pray with him and get him restored to the place in faith he needs to be."

Friar Tomas seemed nervous to meet for the first time with Friar James, but it seemed that everything would go well because of the kindness showed to him by all the other friars. They seemed to genuinely want to help him.

Danica raised her hand to say hello to Friar James as she mused to herself, *It looks like these friars understand what Friar Tomas is going through. It's almost as if they've been there, done that. Oh well, I hope they help him.*

.   By that evening it was becoming apparent to Friar James that Danica and Elkanah were in an absolute relationship and the friar seemed pleased by this. He had seen the two of them holding hands earlier that evening after the prayers and meal. They had been out walking in the cool evening near the chapel, and he saw Elkanah reach down and give Danica a short kiss on the lips. The friar smiled to see that Danica welcomed his kiss and thought they were a good match.

The next day they lingered at the mission a little while longer before leaving because they didn't want the girls and boy to get too exhausted traveling. Besides that, the girls and boy had struck up a great friendship with the friar and he actually had them outside watching him fly his kites that he had made. He seemed to enjoy the much-needed company as much as they needed his friendship and prayers. When it was time for them to leave, he said his prayers for them again to have a safe return home and from his sad countenance it was clear that he felt sure he would never see them again. He was clearly a lonely man.

Elkanah decided on an even longer route back to Jonathan's because he didn't want the boy and girls to see the horrific images at the massacre site where there would surely be the remains of dead bodies.

He had let Danica know this early that morning before leaving the mission. "We will again be going another way that is longer so we can avoid the sights of the massacre where you picked up your bow. By now the buzzards and wild dogs have feasted on the bodies there and the bones and remains will be too ghastly for the young ones to see, but you might like the way we will be going. This is where a lot of trading takes place and you will be able to get the fragrant oils that you and Fleur like so much."

"Will I be able to trade my other Panther fur for it?"

Elkanah nodded.

"Cool."

"Cool what?" He looked puzzled.

"Nothing, just cool." She smiled teasing him.

It took half a day to get to the seaside area where the trading took place between rows and rows of man dug canals. It was impressive to see canoes make their way between these canals as their owners bartered for goods. There were vegetables and seafood of almost every kind and to Danica's amazement, some of the men were actually getting their hair partially shaved and adorned with stylish fabrics and feathers.

"What the heck?" She said as they passed that sight.

"Over there," Elkanah said and pointed, "is where you will find the fragrant oils. Just ask them if they will trade it for your Panther fur. They will see how lustrous and good it is." They made their way over to the oils and Elkanah interpreted as quickly as Danica spoke. This made it extremely easy to communicate and barter. She walked away with the much-desired oils for the fragrant soap that Fleur would make.

They were able to rest there for the night in the safety of the others and the hospitality surprised her. They rested for a while in the congregating area where there were roughly carved benches throughout the entire trading area, and there was plenty of good food everywhere. Later, they had tiny, but comfortable huts for the night. Danica was touched by the care and thoughtfulness that Elkanah showed Irene, Charm and Robby because he knew they would probably not make the duration of the journey back if he hurried them.

It was dark by the time they made it back into the settlement where Fleur and Jonathan lived, but the delay had come about when an old woman approached them on the trail before they reached the settlement. It turned out to be the same old woman they had seen the day Danica had picked up the Spaniard's bow and arrows. The old woman had a wild expression in her eyes and looked out of control. This alarmed Danica at first, but Elkanah assured her that it was okay to deal with her. She had scraggly long hair and was unkempt. It soon became obvious to Danica that she was completely and permanently nuts.

"It's Anna and she just wants pelts." Elkanah walked over to the old woman and handed her a pelt, but Anna just lingered there and was curious about the boy and girls. She seemed to be most interested in their frayed clothing.

Finally, she started walking away and Danica asked, "Why doesn't she just go into the settlement where she can be taken care of?"

"She will never go into any village or settlement. She was once accused of doing devil magic and being a witch, so she ran from the accusers and hid in the woods. She eventually made her way here. I don't know exactly where she came from; no one knows for sure, but some say that she came here a long time ago the same way you did. "

"Too bad, do you think she will talk to me? Maybe I can find out where she came from." Danica was saddened to know that Anna was living in the woods all alone.

"Anna!" Danica shouted and ran to catch up with her.

Anna turned to see what Danica wanted and she seemed surprised to hear someone say her name after so many years.

"Can I talk to you? I'm just wondering where you came from and can I help you to get back home?" Danica could tell by the blank look in Anna's eyes that it was too late for anyone to help her get back home. Her mind had been gone for a long time and it wasn't coming back.

Anna didn't even answer her; she just walked off.

Danica hurried to catch up with the others and Elkanah asked, "How did it go? What did she say?"

"Nothing. I couldn't get her to say anything. Her mind is clearly gone."

They picked up their pace walking because it was getting dark and the girls were exhausted. When they got back into the settlement it was a happy reunion, and they were all made to feel welcome. A rush of warmth and affection swept over Danica as she entered the doorway to Jonathan's and Fleur's small home. Straightway Fleur brought out smoked ham and sweet potatoes along with some hot tea.

Later, Jonathan followed Fleur back to the kitchen area to get a black skillet filled with some homemade apple pie. He leaned over and whispered in her ear with a little laugh, "Did you see how Elkanah and Danica are looking at each other? I don't think she wants to kill him anymore."

Fleur giggled. "No, quite the contrary." Fleur served the apple pie with a smile.

"I was so worried about you, but I knew you would be fine with Elkanah to take care of you." Fleur's tinkling voice made Danica smile too. Fleur turned to Irene and Charm and then sweetly said, "Come sit over here beside me so we can get to know each other." She pointed to some quilts she had spread out on the floor for resting.

Mary, Fleur's daughter, shyly came closer to the girls and sat down with them on the quilts. She showed them the pretty doll that her grandfather, Jonathan's father had bartered from the Europeans. It wasn't long before Irene and Charm were both telling her all about the dolls they had as little girls. The giggling was sweet and refreshing to Danica's ears.

She also saw that Robby was laughing and playing with a spinning top that Jonathan had made out of wood. It had a string firmly wrapped around it and Robby and Ephraim were taking turns spinning it. This did Danica's heart good to see Robby relaxing and having fun.

"Here, you do it!" Robby laughed and handed the top to Elkanah to spin.

"Are you sure you want me to do this?" Elkanah light-heartedly said back.

"Yes!" Robby said.

Danica watched in fascination as Elkanah dramatically wrapped the string around the top to spin it. He looked at Robby and said again, "And you're sure you want me to do this?"

"Yes, do it!" He said louder now.

Elkanah slipped the loop of the string over his middle finger with the fixed tip of the top pointing up and in a flash the top was spinning out and hit the floor. It never tilted to either side. Elkanah let it spin a few seconds and then he reached down and let the spinning top move over into his open palm, and then he let it spin up his left arm and back into his hand again.

They were all laughing by now and they were all clearly amused.

"Wow!" Danica laughed. "That was on fire!"

CHAPTER 20

The next day, Fleur kept the girls and boy there with her for more rest and nourishment. She boiled blackberries, garlic and ginger with a touch of honey for them to sip on. Fleur realized their need for added nourishment and made a large pot of soup with lots of vegetables from her garden. The carrots were cut into large pieces and were delicious.

Later that afternoon, Elkanah and Danica left the children there playing with Fleur's and Jonathan's children while they set out for the tree hut to retrieve her cell phone. The children were all delightfully playing with the top again. It wasn't an easy task trying to explain the cell phone concept to Elkanah, but she tried. Tresla had told Danica that it was important to have every item in her pockets that she had on her when she came through.

Rose Marie was excited to see Danica again and wanted to play. After a few hugs and a banana, Rose Marie took off to play elsewhere, and then Danica and Elkanah settled back into each other's arms and just held each other close and talked for a long time.

"Tell me again, what exactly did Tresla tell you?"

"She told me to make sure I have everything in my pockets that I had when I came through. I can only assume that she meant to make sure I have the right object on my body. It's probably the pendant, but she did say that I have to find the owner of the other half of the pendant and then he would have to release me."

"And there's no other way?" he asked.

"Not that I know of. It's probably a myth anyway," she said.

"I don't know Danica. It's probably true. Let me see it."

She unzipped the pocket of her frayed cargo pants and pulled the pendant out to show Elkanah, "Here it is."

He looked at it in shock and sit up straight. "Danica!" He took it out of her hands and looked closer with surprise. "Look at this!" He pulled the exact mate from inside his tunic. "They match Danica–I lost this at the river the day I pulled you into my canoe. This is what brought you to me," he said in disbelief.

Danica had not even seen his pendant while they were caught up in their lovemaking a few days before. "It's you?" Danica couldn't hide the shock, and then the pleasure and happiness she was feeling at the moment. "It's true then? But how?"

"It's true Danica, and I don't know how, but that's how my father came to my mother. She lost her pendant and he found it. I need the other half of my heart Danica, and that's you. It's not a myth."

They held each other tighter than before and spent the night in the trees, under the stars. They were enjoying just talking and being alone.

The next morning, they discussed it more at length. "What are we going to do? I don't want to leave you, but I have to get the others back and then there is my grandpa and my cousin." She was still trying to process this and make sense of it all.

"I will have to tell you that it is okay for you to go so you will be released to go back, and then it will be your free choice if you decide to come back here and to me."

"You mean that I can choose to come back, and do you release me?" she said.

"Yes, I do release you because I want you to come back to me because you want to, but Danica, when I go back to my mother's village there will surely be an even larger battle than the one you participated in. Tah-Yah-Kee and many of his warriors will join forces with my mother's village to fight this warring tribe north of us. They've sided up with the Spaniards against us in hopes of getting gold and silver for the Spaniards. Many will die. We have to push them back because if we don't, they will kill many more from our villages. They are not good people and want us dead. They also want our horses. And don't you remember that I told you about it. How they think we have large amounts of gold? We really do not."

She knew that what he said was true because of the history of Florida and most of his people were going to be wiped out, except for the one's that may have blended in with the Creeks, Cherokees or others in neighboring states. "What do we do about it? How will I know if you survive?"

"Perhaps I can leave a sign or something to show you if I survive," he said.

"But what?" She buried her face in his chest and was on the verge of tears by now at the thoughts of losing him.

"Do you think you would recognize certain areas of the river where you lived in your time?" he asked.

"I'm not sure."

"Danica, do you remember where I pulled you from the river?"

"Yes, that's the place where I thought you were surely going to kill me." She made a joke about it.

He pulled her close to him. "Never."

"I know that now, but I was truly terrified then."

"I know." He held her tighter to him. "We'll go to the area where I pulled you from the river and then try to remember if you lived north or south from that spot."

"It was definitely south of there."

After a long silence, Elkanah offered a solution that would probably work. "If we take some pottery and bury some items in a place that you recognize and know, then maybe it will still be there in your time."

"I'll put my cell phone in there too."

"But, Tresla said to keep all items on you," Elkanah said.

"I'm going to risk it. How else will I prove to my grandpa that I was really here? Nobody's going to believe this."

"True, and if it doesn't work, well then, we can try it again another way," he said. "Also, if I survive, I'll dig it up and put one of my silver armbands in there, and then you will know for sure that I'm still here. But Danica, we have to go ahead and bury it, with the phone, in case I don't come back. If I don't live, there will be no armband there but your grandpa will still see the phone and know that you were here. It will prove one way or the other, if I live or not. But, I promise you, that I'll be waiting for you–we have to believe this."

She felt sick thinking about it. She nodded and said, "Yes, we have to."

"I know where to get the items we need," he said. "Let's go do it."

Danica and Elkanah carved their names and the year deeply into a piece of clay pottery and partially filled it with oyster shells. She wrapped her cell phone in several pieces of thick leather and placed it on top of the oyster shells, and then Elkanah placed a large, silver medallion wrapped in another piece of leather next to her cell phone. They carefully packed more oyster shells around these two items.

They placed more oyster shells into a larger piece of pottery along with some small rocks and then placed the smaller piece of pottery inside the larger one with more shells on top of this; they sealed it the best they could. Danica knew that leather was organic and would not last over time, but she thought that with it sealed up it might help to preserve the items a little.

"Let's go," he said and they headed for the river and to the exact spot where he pulled her into his canoe.

Her compass pointed them towards the south. "The river is winding, but still, it can be in no other direction," she said.

They canoed the narrow, winding river until they came to a broader and straighter passage that Danica thought looked familiar and was almost certain she recognized it as one of the areas where a bridge had been. The river twisted and turned some more and they saw much floating plant life and Hydrilla growing up from the bottom of the river in the shallow water. She felt that they were getting closer to where she had lived with her grandfather.

"Look," Danica pointed ahead to a much broader area of open water where a park had been located in her time. "I'm positive this is the place where a park was."

"A park?"

"Yes, a place where you can go to relax with other people to walk or play," she said.

"It sounds a little like our festivals," he said.

"Not exactly a festival, but it is for fun and relaxation."

"Oh, okay."

Finally, she spotted an area that she was certain was where her grandfather's house had been in her time. It wasn't overgrown with weeds like Danica thought it might be, but instead, the dirt was pressed down from people making frequent trips to the river to put their canoes in and to fish. Luckily for Danica and Elkanah, not one single person was in sight. She quickly spotted the large rocks that were down at the end of her grandpa's property, beside the shed. They pulled the canoe out of the water and went over to the place where her grandpa's shed would have been.

"Here, right over here is where the shed was."

Elkanah said, "Okay, let's bury these and after the battle I'll dig this up and add my arm band to this so you'll know that I'm waiting here for you. And Danica I'm going to come here daily and stand right here on this very spot where you will be. I'll be thinking of you. And in the evenings, I will be waiting by the river where you first came through and I'll be looking for you." He spread his hands. "I'm just trying to make it work."

"I'll do the same." She promised.

They buried it about two feet deep and left to go back for the girls and boy and to say goodbye to Fleur and Jonathan. It wasn't that easy, but she knew what she had to do.

They explained everything to the girls and boy and then took them to the exact spot where Elkanah had pulled her from the water. Elkanah and Danica just lingered there holding each other tight. He kissed her the final time and said, "Danica, promise me that you'll come back to me."

She couldn't hold back the tears. "I promise you that I'll come back. I love you.

"I love you too," and he said again, "Danica, come back to me." His eyes had that troubled look again as Danica, Irene, Charm and Robby held each other tight and fell over into the dark river.

For just one fleeting moment, Danica knew she saw Tresla swimming near them and then Tresla spoke to her. *"As I told you, I swim in the springs that go for miles underground and I want my energy to energize this water here to make it possible for you to go back to your time. If there is not enough energy here, the timing will be off and that could be disastrous for you all. I'll also keep these waters energized for you in case you want to come back, and Danica, don't forget to look up because when you get back to your time I will already be back in place with the other stars. I will be smiling at you."*

Danica and the others had a firm grip on each other and with a swoosh they felt a strong current sweep them away and through space-time from 1624 to the year 2017. They saw the blue lights as they slipped **under the blue rainbow** together and back to their time and place.

255

CHAPTER 21

They all came up and out of the water at the same time gasping for air.

"Swim! Get to shore!" Danica yelled at all of them. Robby surprised her and made it on his own to some boaters that were fishing near the edge of the riverbank. Other boaters helped the girls to safety.

The boaters saw that they were clearly in distress and called 911. Danica explained to deputies about her canoeing accident and what had taken place after that. It sounded to the officers like she was rambling, especially when she mentioned the caverns.

Robby, Irene and Charm also tried to explain what had happened to them and how Danica had helped them through the forest and then home. Robby told the officers how Danica had rescued him from the awful men and how she had given him food and water. He told them about the campfires she had made and kept him warm. They were astonished to hear that she had carried him for days through the forest and even killed a Panther that had almost attacked him. They were even more puzzled when he told them about the cave with the other children and how he had played in the pool of water with them.

Likewise, Irene and Charm told the officers about Chua and his warriors keeping them tied up and the atrocities that had been committed against them. They told about how Danica had found them tied up at the back of the camp and cut their ropes to free them. It appeared to the officers that some real bad criminals were living in the woods and terrorizing people. They came to the conclusion that the real bad men had kidnapped them all and may be holding more children captive.

After piecing the information together, the officers assumed that Danica managed to escape her kidnapper and then rescued the others. It was also assumed that they had wandered for miles through the forest near an Indian Reservation or perhaps a Pow wow festival with storytelling, crafts, dancing, flutes and drums, etc. where they had received some help. It was puzzling, but they knew that the debriefing would reveal a lot more in time.

It wasn't very long before news crews were out and wanting statements. Cameras were everywhere and onlookers were trying to push through the crowds to find out more details. The sheriff's department was doing their best to investigate the situation and find out who those awful men were that had obviously kidnapped them. It was assumed that these kidnappers overpowered them while they were at a disadvantage after their canoes had turned over.

Danica's grandpa just happened to be watching the news and when he saw them interviewing Danica, he called Josh in disbelief. The tightness in his chest left him a little breathless and he knew it wasn't a good sign. At least the dizziness went away and he left as soon as Josh and Jordan got there to pick him up. They rushed to Danica as quickly as possible. Danica saw her grandpa's white T-shirt first, and then she saw him shuffling as fast as he could, making sobbing sounds as he hurriedly moved towards her. The whole thing was overwhelming and they were all in tears, but it was sheer joy to be together again.

They were all taken to the hospital for observation and the doctors took them through mental and physical health exams looking for trauma. Long-term counseling was recommended to treat the girls and boy for post-traumatic stress and to give them time to talk through their trauma and to regain a sense of safety to reunite with their families.

It was in the news for days about Danica Larsen, Army veteran and granddaughter to Augustus (Gus) Larsen, retired Navy SEAL, and how she courageously rescued the young people from some real bad kidnappers who had kept them in the forest for months. Everyone around town was talking about the young woman who had been the guard to a chaplain in Afghanistan and who was now considered a hero.

Phone calls came in like crazy to Gus and Danica from people they knew, and from people that just wanted to congratulate her and to tell Gus how brave they thought Danica was for saving the lives of those young people. The parents of the young ones were eternally grateful and expressed that on the news that same day they returned.

Gus couldn't hide the pride he felt for her. Danica smiled and thought, *you just don't know. I was terrified.*

After a few weeks, things settled down for Danica and she began to open up to her grandpa about what had really happened while she was away. It wasn't that he didn't believe her, but he thought the trauma was working a number on her and confusing her. He gently insisted that she continue the counseling at the VA hospital for a while. It didn't take long for her to realize that the therapist didn't believe the things she told him about Elkanah, and he thought she was suffering from post-traumatic stress disorder from things she had heard and seen in Afghanistan. He really thought she was looney when she told him about Tresla, the star.

When she came out of her counseling session, her grandpa asked how it went.

She said in a slightly irritated way, "Those fuckers think I'm crazy."

"Honey, nobody thinks you're crazy; you just went through a frightening ordeal and stress can do weird stuff to you." Her grandpa hugged her. "You'll get through this okay, you'll see."

"They asked me if I wanted to go into the hospital on a voluntary basis and I said, 'hell no'. Those fuckers think I'm delusional. Anyway, they said if I go to the hospital, they can evaluate me and get me on meds. And, they want my medical records from the Army. Those shit heads can kiss my fucking ass."

"Well, try to not let it upset you." Gus saw that Danica was clearly agitated and he was a little amused at her words knowing that she had learned to curse like that from him.

"Those assholes." She was still disgusted.

A few weeks went by and Danica started wondering if everybody was correct in their assessment of her because all of this did sound nuts, but Elkanah had been so real to her. She didn't want to admit to anyone that she still felt haunted by the thoughts of him and his love making. She would go out every day and just stand where he had stood beside the shed. Her heart yearned for his love and his gentle touch, but with time, she decided that it must be just a fantasy.

She went through the motions of going to the shooting range and other things, but her heart was just not in it. She grew listless and depressed. The doctor assured her that this would soon pass and she would get back to normal. In the meantime, the doctor was trying to get her onto disability and that pissed her off even more.

Danica and her grandpa grilled out often with Jordan, Josh, their parents, and a few others that wanted to come. No special invitation was needed, just show up, and then guess who walked in the door acting as if he had done nothing wrong at all. Yes, it was Alex.

Right away Alex ran over to Danica, hugged her and said, "Danica, I was so worried about you and I hope you're not still mad at me. I'll pay you back. I promise."

She had to roll her eyes at that. "No, I'm not mad at you anymore. You're a knucklehead, but I'm not mad at you. And you do need to get a grip on that gambling."

"Yeah, yeah, I'm working on it."

"I'll bet you are. I'm sure you go to the casino every day."

"Well, not every day," he said.

She turned to Josh and forced a smile. "See, I didn't bury him in the backyard after all."

Josh laughed and said, "You should have."

"I know." She said and they all turned and gave Alex a teasing look that said 'we might kill you'.

They all laughed at this and Josh said to Danica, "I'm just kidding. I never thought you did."

"But, don't be so sure I wouldn't." Danica just shook her head and gave Alex that teasing look again.

"I swear. I'll pay you back."

"Well okay, but hey, go grab a beer," she said to Alex and then motioned towards a tub filled with ice, beer, water and sodas.

"Cool, but where's the homemade wine? I want some of that."

"Oh, it's over there." She nonchalantly pointed towards a table near the glass doors.

"I love this stuff," he said pouring a rather large glass of wine for himself.

"I'll bet you do. It is pretty good." Danica suppressed a giggle and turned her head so Alex wouldn't see the amused look on her face. "Everyone does love Grandpa's wine, but be careful, it'll knock you on your butt."

He took a sip of it and smiled.

She turned her attention back to Jordan. "So, what did you buy in Atlanta this time?"

"You wouldn't believe the designer jeans I bought, and I found the cutest tee-shirts to go with them. I brought you one."

"Cool! Let's see it."

"Hold on, let me get it." Jordan headed back into the living room where she had left two large shopping bags. Shopping was the one thing that got her motor running, and in high gear.

"Here, what do you think?" She held up a black rhinestone embellished tee-shirt.

"I love it."

"I thought you would, and get a look at these cashmere sweaters. I'm sure they will sell, and they will look great with the skirts. Even the dresses and jeans, it doesn't matter. Some are baby pinks and blues. And then, my favorite of course, is this white one. Here, feel it."

Danica stroked the soft white sweater and especially liked the dainty turquoise blue and silver buttons. "Nice."

"Look, I found these ribbed crop fit tee-shirts. They come just below the waist." Jordan held up a coral one, then a teal one, and then a yellow one. "I thought they would all three go with the sweater."

Danica said, "They will, and my favorite is the teal."

"And what do you think of these slouch boots to go with the jeans? I like the soft leather and they are a dream to wear. I wore a pair back from Atlanta."

"Oh wow, I'm definitely buying the jeans, boots, and sweater!" Danica smiled and said.

"I thought you would like those, and get a look at this," Jordan was enthusiastically pulling things out of the bag. She now pulled a soft leather hobo looking purse from her shopping bag. "They had these in teal, brown, and red. Of course, they had black and white too. I got all of them. And look at these studded wedge shoes I'm wearing. Do you like these?" Clothes and shoes definitely excited her.

"Dang, what all did you cram into those bags?" Danica giggled at Jordan's enthusiasm over shopping. "Yes, but of course I love those shoes."

Jordan was stuffing things back into the bags and said, "I thought you might want to go to Dallas with me next week. I'm going to a new designer clothing warehouse there. What do you think?"

Josh spoke up then, "I think you should go Danica."

"Maybe. I'll probably go." And Danica thought to herself, *and Jordan, on the airplane maybe I'll tell you about this really funny looking lizard girl that I saw while I was away. I really do want to tell you all about her, but I guess I won't now. I also wanted to tell you about the gator I killed, but it probably didn't happen anyway.* She sighed because when she had told Jordan about Elkanah, she could tell by her silence that she thought she needed to keep seeing the doctor. If she told her about Nolia, or the gator, she would think she was crazy for sure.

"Honey, excuse me. It looks like Grandpa needs help at the grill," Danica said. She saw that Grandpa was trying to cook steaks and shrimp at the same time, and it was a fact that nobody wanted the steaks overdone.

Alex followed Danica out to the lanai and then to the grill. "Can I talk to you?" he said.

Here it comes, Danica thought, and nodded. By now Grandpa had already gone back into the kitchen with the shrimp.

"I'm really sorry I let you down, and I've really missed you. Maybe we can go to a movie later this evening."

Not this again, she thought. "Not this time. I'm really still pretty tired from it all," she said and was glad when her grandpa came back outside and interrupted this conversation that she regarded as nonsense. *It's never gonna happen*, she thought.

CHAPTER 22

That next week they went to Dallas, and Danica wore her new designer jeans with the teal tee-shirt. She carried the white cashmere sweater in case she needed it on the flight. It was not unusual for her to get a little cold while traveling. The turquoise and silver buttons on the sweater matched her skinny silver belt and tiny diamond stud earrings that sparkled in the white gold. She couldn't resist the urge to wear her new slouch boots and took the large hobo look handbag along. She had not been able to resist buying the whole outfit. It was just her style, and Jordan knew exactly what Danica would love. Danica also knew that Jordan wanted to see her happy again.

They caught a cab to the hotel and then they went directly to their rooms. Unpacking wasn't that hard and then they rested some before going to the designer clothing warehouse. Danica touched up her makeup in the cab. She felt a surge of self-confidence as they walked up several steps towards the building. Before they left the hotel, Jordan had curled Danica's hair and she could feel the soft curls bounce when she walked and heard the jingle of her bangle bracelets. She almost felt like she was back to normal, but the thoughts of Elkanah still haunted her. She was doing the best she could to get beyond all of this and go forward, but she had her doubts that she would ever forget him.

It was a fun day with a lot of buying. The gentleman helping them introduced himself as Raphael, and when he spoke, he had a gracious, charming demeanor and Danica immediately felt at ease there.

"Look at this." Raphael held out three different dresses for them both to see. They were exactly Jordan's style, and one was a blush pink lace midi, and one was a lavender lace midi. "Here, feel how soft these two are." After they felt them, he put those down and then held out a light green dress with an elegant and smooth texture. "And ladies, you're going to absolutely love this one. This fabulous rayon mixture will be cool and comfortable for casual daytime wear or for the evenings."

She enjoyed looking at the different styles, and feeling the fabrics that Raphael would suggest. He did have good taste and she understood why Jordan loved buying from him. His clothes were beautiful and he knew exactly what Jordan liked.

Jordan found some women's sports fashions to add to her selection for her shop. She even found some soft peach cold shoulder blouses that were a wee bit pricey, but too cute to pass up. Jordan claimed the lavender Midi A-line lace dress for her very own. It was so flowy and soft with short sleeves. After they left Raphael's, they did some personal shopping for themselves and found some flattering jewelry and other accessories.

Later they had a late lunch at a nearby restaurant that had incredibly good Italian food, and Jordan approached the subject of Danica's future. "You know Danica that my shop is growing and I would like for you to work with me. Will you do that?"

Danica smiled. "I'll think about it." She didn't tell Jordan that she had been thinking about working at the shooting range part-time and would probably be giving shooting lessons. She would also go back to college a couple of nights a week. Danica could tell that it would be quite a decision because she did love clothes and shopping, but she also loved shooting as a recreational sport even more. However, because of her skill at this sport, giving lessons just seemed like the natural thing to do.

Even though she was skilled at using various types of weapons with speed and accuracy, she also knew that going back into the Army was not an option. She was feeling at the moment that she was 'almost' ready to go forward with her life.

After lunch they went to another fashion warehouse that had shoes of every possible style and color.

"Look at this!" Jordan was so excited picking out red glittery shoes, silly shoes with large black bows, sling backs in satin and crystal, black studded clear shoes with wildly, crazy high heels, shoes with straps and buckles around the ankles, and on and on. If the shoes glittered, Jordan wanted them.

"Wow, I love those! All of them." Danica giggled and knew that these were all the things about Jordan that she would never change.

That evening they had a nice dinner in a high-end steak house that was highly recommended, and the wine strangely reminded her of the wine that Friar James had given to her while she was at the mission. Jordan managed to get her attention back to the present by discussing each and every piece of clothing, shoes, and jewelry they had purchased that day. Jordan's bubbly sweetness and enthusiasm about the clothes made Danica smile. Jordan just couldn't stop talking about clothes and Danica thought that was *alright* because that was what was so cute about her. They all loved Jordan for 'just being Jordan' and nobody wanted to change her. At least she was cheerful, optimistic, and fun to be around.

After that, they were exhausted, so they headed back to their hotel rooms to rest for the evening before their trip back to Tampa. They had to be at the airport the following morning by 7:45am. It was a great trip and Jordan's shop was a big success because of Jordan's taste for cute clothes.

CHAPTER 23

Several days went by and things didn't get better for Danica; she was slipping back into a depression. She walked over to the park just trying to clear her head, and all she could think about was Elkanah and his kisses. She remembered the day they had canoed down this very river trying to locate where grandpa's house should be, and it just confused her even more, so she headed on back home. When she reached the backyard, she looked over at the shed and thought she heard Elkanah's voice saying to her, "Danica, come back to me." She shook her head and thought, *no, it can't be, and his arm band can't really be there. I have to get a grip*, and she walked back to the house.

"You look a little down," Grandpa said when she came in.

"Grandpa, I'm trying to get my thoughts straight, but Grandpa, I know he was real and there was this old woman named Anna. Elkanah told me that some say she got there the same way I did. It's just puzzling about her though."

Her grandpa looked at her with a strange look and said, "There was a woman named Anna a long time ago that turned up missing.

She was never found, but it couldn't possibly be her. It was so long ago."

Danica remembered the way Anna had curiously looked at Charm's and Irene's thin and tattered clothing. She had actually touched the fabric of the boy's shirt and seemed confused by it all before she ran off.

"Anyway honey, it'll take time, you'll see." Her grandpa tried hard to make her feel better.

"Grandpa, remember I told you about the large battle that Elkanah told me about?"

"Yes."

"He said if he survived, he would bury one of his arm bands under the shed. Don't you remember that I told you how we canoed here that day to see where the house was located."

"Yes, I remember."

"We buried things there to prove that all of this did happen," she said, "even my cell phone is in there."

"Honey, there's nothing there. I put that shed there myself before you were ever born. I cleared this lot myself and poured the slab of concrete where the shed is. I even poured the patio myself. Nothing's there Danica."

Danica felt saddened by this and said, "I guess you're right."

"You'll get over all of this. Don't you remember what the doctors said? It's all part of the trauma. Honey, don't you remember how the doctor explained that because of the trauma your mind could possibly go somewhere else to deal with it, just to cope with the situation. That's all. You'll heal in time," he said.

"I guess. Oh well, anyway, I'm tired and I just feel like resting for a while." She was exhausted a lot these days and even though the trip to Dallas was nice, it didn't help a lot. She just didn't feel ready to make a decision yet, and her heart still grieved for Elkanah.

When she got to her room, she stared at the water bottle that she still had from the canoeing accident. It was especially useful in the forest, and she would refill it every chance she got. She remembered that the last time she had filled it was from the spring of water at the cave when she was there to see Tresla. Her compass was there too, along with the bird pendant. She pondered over this for a long time remembering her cell phone that she had buried in the pottery where the shed is now, beside the large rocks.

The next day she was just resting in the recliner and watching the news. It seemed that there was nothing on except terrorist attacks and random killings. It depressed her even more. She thought, *hell, what's worse? This nothing bullshit here, or what's back there in Elkanah's world?*

When her grandpa shuffled into the room she said, "Grandpa, I just can't do this anymore. I know it was real, and people there were bathing in a spring and their aches and pains would go away. And now it makes me wonder if it really was the legendary fountain of youth that Ponce de Leon searched for."

"What? How can that be?"

"I'm not sure, but I'm wondering if it really did exist back then, but now it has almost diminished over time. That's why nobody can find it. Maybe there was a cataclysmic event that caused it to happen back then, but now it has almost ceased to exist. And maybe Tresla's energy really did cause the fountain of youth to make people feel younger and stronger, but now her energy is almost gone. I don't know, just maybe."

"Baby, you've got to let it go," he kindly said.

"I can't grandpa, and don't you remember what I told you about Tresla? She said she was from the Sagittarius Arm and for me to look up in the summer months and she would be smiling at me. And grandpa, we buried things under the shed to prove all of this. We buried a piece of pottery with our names and the year 1624 engraved on it. I put my cell phone in there with other things. I have to know if Elkanah lived. Grandpa, I have to know. He said he would put his armband beside my cell phone if he survived. I have to know for sure, one way or the other. If he lived, I can go back and have him gradually remove his people to other places so they can blend in with other tribes and possibly survive what is surely to come for them here. They will all be wiped out if they stay where they are."

"Okay Danica, you'll never get peace until you see for yourself that there's nothing there."

"Thank you, Grandpa. I have to know," she said with gratitude in her voice.

"I know you do, but you do know how much junk is in that shed."

"Yes, I know."

"Anyway, the shed is old and it's on that slab of concrete. I'll have to get a new one and clean this old one out and throw most of the junk out for the garbage man. Better yet, let's just have the handyman and his helper do it. He can dismantle the old one and remove the slab of concrete. Then we can dig under it so you can see for yourself that nothing is there."

After the new shed was installed beside the old one, it didn't take long for the handyman and his helper to clean out the old one and dismantle it. Danica was eager to get this over with and so was her grandpa, to make it possible for her to get closure and go on with her life.

"Come on Grandpa, I'll dig," Danica said. "I have to be careful and not break the pottery."

"Okay." He said humoring her and she knew it.

As it turned out, it was not that easy to find the right spot, but she kept digging, and digging and found nothing.

"Come on honey, it's getting dark. We'll dig some more tomorrow."

She was disappointed but reluctantly gave up her search for that day. The next day she searched with a metal detector and it picked up nothing. She dug again until she was exhausted, and then her grandpa helped dig.

"Honey, it's just not here," her grandpa said.

She couldn't hold back the tears. "I guess not." They both sadly walked back into the house.

That night she couldn't stop thinking about it and in her mind, she carefully retraced each step she had taken with Elkanah that day. They had counted their steps and that's why she thought it should be under the shed. But, *I wonder,* she thought, *if erosion caused the landscape to change in certain places, then it might not be under the shed.*

She told her grandpa what she realized and he said, "Could be. Let's just go buy a real good metal detector and get rid of this old one." He wanted her to finally have closure over this obsession, once and for all.

They scanned the whole backyard and picked up a few junk finds. Soda tabs, pennies, and an old horse bit. "Where did that come from?" she said and laughed.

"No telling what was here before I moved here."

She wouldn't give up and to her relief the metal detector picked up something again. She dug carefully and her shovel hit something. She thought, *please be there*. She knew that something was definitely there, but what. She was nowhere near where the shed had been; she was digging over closer to the fence and under some overgrown shrubs. She managed to get the dirt from around the object so she could safely pull it up and out of the ground. She let out an excited yell, "Grandpa, it's here." Under her breath she said, "Please God, let his arm band be there."

"It is here!" Her grandpa said in amazement. "And I planted those shrubberies there myself years ago."

"I told you it would be here." She took it over to the wooden picnic table to clean off the hard-packed dirt and then carefully started taking oyster shells out of the pottery. Her heart was pounding and she said again, "Please God, let him be alive."

Grandpa said, "Here." He had brought her some wet rags to gently remove the dirt.

She carefully removed oyster shells and rocks one by one, and then lifted the smaller pot out of the larger one. It was unbelievable, but it was still fully intact. The leather didn't last over time, but their names and dates were there. Her heart was rapidly beating as she removed more oyster shells from the smaller pot, one by one. She stopped for a minute to brace herself in case there was no armband. She reached into the smaller pot again. Now with trembling hands, she touched something dirty and square; it was her cell phone. "Look Grandpa, my cell phone."

"Let me see." Grandpa reached for the phone in disbelief. "I can't believe this!"

She was sweating now and her head felt heavy. She felt another anxiety attack coming on but she took some deep breaths and reached into the pot again. She felt dizzy but forced herself to move her hand around and then she touched something. She drew her hand back and then reached inside the pot again. There were two items there – she pulled one of the items out and let out a short scream.

She couldn't hold back the tears. "It's here Grandpa. He's alive." She held up his armband and then reached into the pottery again and pulled out his other armband. "They're both here Grandpa. He wants me to come to him. I'm going Grandpa. Come with me. You can bathe in the energized water and feel better. Those people that bathe in the water don't live forever, but they live without pain as long as Tresla's energy remains there. She explained to me that her energy will slowly decline over time after she leaves there, but for now, they are out of pain."

He looked stunned.

"I'm going back."

"I don't know what to say," he said.

"I do. You want to quit hurting, don't you? Come with me. We can leave this silver medallion here and a letter for Josh and Jordan explaining all of this. When we get there, I'll bury my new cell phone and a piece of my jewelry under Josh's patio so they can dig it up and then they will believe all of this. They can use the medallion to come too if they want to, and Grandpa, there's the bottle of water upstairs that came from the cave. It has energized water in it. Sponge that onto your hands and knees to strengthen you so you can go through. Let me go get it."

"Okay."

Immediately his hands and feet quit aching and that was enough to convince him that he wanted to go with Danica. They wrote the letter in great detail and left it on the kitchen table for Josh and Jordan, with clear instructions. She explained about the erosion along the river that would take place over time and told them to keep looking for the cell phone until they find it.

Danica put her bird pendant and compass into her pocket. She put both of Elkanah's armbands into another pocket and put the canoe into the river. They went to the very spot where she had had the other canoeing accident and this time it was easy. She held tight to her grandpa as they fell over into the water, and immediately, they saw the layers of blue forming. It happened just like before with the first layer of blue, and then the next, and next until they finally slipped **under the blue rainbow.**

In an instant, time was turning back to the year 1624. As soon as they came up and out of the water, Danica could hear her grandpa gasping for air. He immediately felt better because of Tresla's energy that was still there in the water. He felt so good that he took off running as soon as he made it to the riverbank, and he was stronger now than he had been in his youth.

When Danica went through, she landed face down in the shallow edge of the riverbank and felt a little frightened at first, that is until she smelled that familiar smell of oily pelts and Elkanah's buckskins. She looked around and knew he must be near. She heard a slight movement through the bushes and suddenly he was there. The musky scent was so close now, and the sound of breaking twigs told her that he was right there in her presence.

Her heart was beating fast as he approached her. She could hear him moving through the shrubs and bushes as fast as he could towards her. The bushes parted and she saw his moccasins first, then the way his loose-fitting buckskins moved around his thighs as he walked swiftly towards her. Her eyes moved up to his multi colored shirt and then to his face that was eagerly searching for her. It melted her heart to have him so near and at the same time they reached out for each other and touched.

She said, "I knew you would be here."

"I knew you would come too." He took her into his arms and said, "I'll never let you go."

CHAPTER 24

The next day Josh couldn't reach Danica or their grandpa by phone and the front door was locked. "This is just too weird," Josh said to Jordan. "I wonder where they are? The truck's not here."

"Let's go around back," Jordan suggested and was already headed that way as she was speaking. The high shrubberies blocked the view of the backyard from the other yards, but once they were past those, Jordan sucked in her breath. "Oh no, what in the world happened to this backyard?"

"What the heck?" Josh almost yelled.

"Grandpa, where are you? Danica?" Josh pulled open the screen door to the back lanai and not a soul was there. They didn't waste any time heading into the kitchen. "Grandpa. Danica, where are you."

"Look at this." Jordan was the first to see Danica's letter telling them about finding the buried pots in the backyard, and Elkanah's arm bands. "Listen to this," Jordan started to read the letter out loud to Josh. "The pots are in the backyard to prove to you that what I said is the truth. Take Elkanah's medallion and if you two decide to join us, you can. I've clearly explained here how you do it. The proof with my cell phone is under your patio or close by. Just keep looking, it's there. I love you both. Danica."

THE END

Thank you to my husband, Larry Silver LCSW, for his advice about PTSD and depression that helped me to understand what Danica dealt with after her return from the forest.

CITE - I would like to make mention of the credible sources I have used in my research to write She Slipped UNDER THE BLUE RAINBOW. First of all, THE STORY IS FICTION and only intended to entertain.

University of West Florida-Luna Settlement.

University of South Florida – Jean Ribault.

University of Florida – Banana Growing in the Florida Home Landscape by Jonathan H. Crane and Carlos F. Balerdi. Been around Florida since the Spaniards and Portuguese brought in 16th century.

The Archivo General de Indias. Seville, Spain. MASKS.

Inweekly - African Presence.

Wikipedia – Calusa -- Luna Expedition.

Wikipedia –History of North Carolina, Juan Pardo, explorer1560 and Sir Walter Raleigh, namesake of city of Raleigh 1580.

Wikipedia-Reptilian humanoid used in fantasy/Sc-Fi.

Huguenots in the United States Genealogy – Church Records South Carolina – Jean Ribault established a French Huguenot colony in South Carolina in 1562.

Florida – From South Carolina, French Huguenots led by Rene Goulaine de Laudonniere settle in Florida in 1564.

Hernando de Escalante Fontaneda memoirs.Archivo General de Indias.

He was enslaved by the Calusas for 17 years and spoke several languages. Also, Indian Traders often had Indian wives and children. I'm sure the children learned the language of both parents. People have always been known to adapt to other people's environments, including their language.

His memoirs also makes mention of the mythical Fountain of Youth and Juan Ponce de Leon.

He also makes mention of MASKS

(The Spaniards witnessed elaborate rituals with synchronized singing and processions of MASKED priests. Inside a great temple, they observed walls covered by carved and painted wooden MASKS.)

Wikipedia – Calusa – MASKS
(Calusa ceremonies included processions of priests and singing women. The priests wore carved MASKS, which were at other times hung on the walls inside a temple.
The African Presence in "America's First Settlement" published in (inweekly Pensacola).
Tristan de Luna colony in Pensacola, 1559. Some were enslaved.
Black Panther vs Cougar? See Tracking The Carrabelle Cat:
Florida's black panther mystery. Who really knows for sure.
John H. Hann and Jacques Le Moyne

Made in the USA
Monee, IL
26 October 2023

45200753R00173